**A billionaire bounty hunter n
vows to capture her heart.**

No woman has ever held Carter Eckhouse's heart until he meets Jo Hollander. Their hot hookups have him begging for more. There's just one problem...she's on his warrant list and he has to take her in or lose his professional reputation.

Oh yeah, and his best friend has declared his girlfriend's sister off-limits.

Things are about to get messy.

If you like bad boys, billionaires, and steamy sex, you won't want to miss this standalone story by multiple award-winning author Jeana E. Mann.

PRETTY BROKEN BASTARD

JEANA E. MANN

ISHKADIDDLE PUBLISHING

CHAPTER 1

CARTER

For the better part of a year, I'd been tailing Clarence Mortimer Benson III. And, for the better part of a year, I'd always been ten steps behind, ten minutes too late, or ten blocks away from capturing him. His girlfriend lived in the building across from a small independent coffee shop, so I started hanging out in the neighborhood, hoping to catch a glimpse of him. The ten-thousand-dollar bond on his head kept me focused.

From my seat on the bench across the street, I stared through the window of Joe's Java Junction. The petite barista inside kept stealing my attention. Jo Hollander, bustled behind the counter, confident and commanding. Damn, I loved a self-assured woman. The tail of her long brown ponytail twitched as she moved between the cash register and the espresso machine. It wasn't her hair that had me mesmerized. It was those tits. Big, bouncy, and too large for her tiny frame, they taunted me from a dozen yards away. I dreamed about those breasts at night, taking them in my hands, sucking her...

I cut myself off. Hell, it didn't matter what I thought. She was absolutely, undeniably, one hundred percent off-limits. At least, that was what my best friend, Rhett, said. The temptation of forbidden fruit made her even more attractive. Normally, I'd have blown off his warning and shagged her in the alley behind the coffee shop or in her apartment elevator or wherever she'd have me. In my opinion, all women were fair game as long as they weren't married. Jo, however, was his future sister-in-law, and Rhett was one of the few people in this world whom I respected. I went along with his request, but it couldn't keep me from spying on her or jacking off in the shower to fantasies of her hot little body.

My phone rang. I hit the accept button. "Hey, Darcy. What's up?"

"One of our tipsters called. Your guy just got on a plane to New York." In the background, her long fingernails clacked on the computer keyboard.

"Shit. This guy is slippery." For a college preppy from old money, Clarence possessed impressive criminal skills. Then again, in my experience, the older the money, the more questionable the morals. Of all people, I should know, coming from a long line of corrupt politicians. I tossed down the magazine I'd been pretending to read. "Get hold of the Brooklyn office. See if they can help us out."

"One step ahead of you, boss." Darcy's quiet efficiency emanated through the phone.

"Have I told you lately how awesome you are?" I smiled at the mental picture of her in the office, dressed in a low-cut top and too-tight pants, her platinum blond hair in some kind of outrageous, elaborate updo.

"Nope. Tell me now." The typing ceased. "Or, instead of words, you could give me a raise. And if that isn't possible, how about a nice couple of weeks in Tahiti?" Her voice lifted hopefully.

"I'll do better than that. If we catch this motherfucker in the next ten days, I'll buy you a new car." Since we'd met, she'd been tooling around town in a geriatric Lincoln Continental held together by duct tape and prayers. "Any car you want."

"Anything I want? *Anything*?" She held her breath.

"Sure. Within reason."

"I'm thinking Mercedes. Convertible. Powder blue." Excitement raised her voice an octave.

"Give me Benson, and we'll talk." I jerked the phone from my ear as her squeal pierced the air waves.

"On it." The phone went dead, and the dial tone buzzed in my ear. That was one of the things I loved best about her. She didn't waste time on words when there was work to be done.

Pocketing my phone, I walked to the intersection. My lips pursed in a tuneless whistle. A pretty redhead gave me the once over. I winked at her, enjoying her smile. Across the street, Jo hung the closed sign in the display window and locked the door. I waited for the light to change so I could cross the street to the nearby parking garage. A few seconds later, a petite blonde emerged from the alley next to the coffee shop wearing dark sunglasses. Jo? I squinted against the bright sunlight. Yes, it was her. She might have hidden her dark hair, but those tits couldn't be denied.

The light changed, and I crossed the street. Jo tucked her chin against her chest and brushed past me. What was she up to? Some kind of kinky role play? Dual identities? No matter what the reason for her costume, Jo Hollander just climbed a few notches on my radar of interest. Unlike most men, I enjoyed a little bit of crazy in my bed. I glanced at my watch, warring between curiosity and responsibility. With three appointments and a court appearance on my calendar, the mystery of Jo Hollander would have to wait until tomorrow.

CHAPTER 2

JO

The bell above the door clanged as morning customers flooded into the cramped coffee shop. Through the steam of the espresso machine, I scanned the faces, nodding to those I knew and giving each one a smile—until the last one. Brown, mischievous eyes met mine over the glass countertop. A shiver ran down my back—the pleasant kind—because those thick-lashed eyes were set into the handsomest face I'd ever seen and attached to a body built for sin. The way he walked, muscles coiled beneath a snug black T-shirt and low-slung camouflage pants, suggested power and confidence and arrogance, all the traits I loved to hate in a man.

This guy, Carter Eckhouse, was no stranger. He was my sister's boyfriend's best friend, and that meant I had to tolerate his childish, misogynistic behavior to keep the family peace. While I bounced between attraction and dislike, one corner of his mouth curled up in an enigmatic grin, inspiring a dozen questions inside my head. Was he laughing at me? His gaze dropped a few inches below my chin then further still. Unnerved, I glanced down to see the swells of my breasts pushing up through the V neck of my T-shirt.

"Dick," I muttered under my breath. *Oh, no.* Heat rushed into my face. Did I really say that out loud? I glanced around, but no one else seemed to have noticed. Business had slowed to a snail's pace. The last thing I needed was to offend the other customers. I loved the coffee shop and the people who visited us every day. Well, everyone but him. Why, why, why did he have to come here? There were dozens of coffee shops in the city. Why mine?

"Nice to see you, too, Jo." His deep, gravelly voice hit low in my belly, the edges of his words rough and teasing. A voice like that was made for hot, dirty talk, the kind that made my panties dampen and my thighs clench.

"Double espresso and a large water, right?" I fought to keep the tremble out of my voice. What was it about him that unsettled me so much? It couldn't have anything to do with the impossible width of his shoulders or the flat stretch of his abdomen underneath that tight T-shirt.

"You know it." Thick brown eyebrows lifted. "I'm surprised you remember."

"It's my job to remember." How could I forget? Twice before, he'd visited with Rhett and Bronte, then several times on his own. Every time he came within ten feet of me, my knees dissolved, and a strange flutter happened in my tummy.

"Keep the change." From his wallet, he withdrew a crisp ten-dollar bill. I stared at his long, calloused fingers, so manly and strong, the bones of his wrist, the thick vein running up his forearm to his swollen bicep. A dull throb blossomed between my legs. He cleared his throat; he was waiting for me to take the money while I drooled on the counter.

"Have a seat. I'll bring it over when it's ready." Most people waited on their order, but I needed to put distance between us before my self-control cracked. I eased the bill from his grasp. His fingers grazed my palm in what might—or might not—have been a deliberate caress. I fought against the prickle of gooseflesh crawling up my arm and stabbed at the cash register with an index finger.

"I'll be right over here. Waiting." That dirty voice curled around the words and curled my toes in the process. He lingered for a moment longer, like he had more to say, before heading to a table by the window.

I braced a hand against the cash register, undone by the strong tug of physical awareness. If I was seriously considering Carter as an end to my sexual drought, I needed an intervention, and fast. His cavalier attitude toward women rubbed me the wrong way. Many times, I'd overheard him bragging about his casual hookups with Rhett. He never bothered to lower his voice, detailing the women like they were prize mares at a horseshow, regaling the impromptu fucks after a night of drinking, the way he left them the second they finished. And once, after I'd argued with Rhett, Carter had propositioned me. *Do you want to angry-fuck?* I'd stuttered an irate refusal, while my womb had rippled at the thought of those big, rough hands on my ass and his narrow hips between my thighs.

"I said mocha latte, not vanilla." Lyle, my assistant manager, pushed the steaming mug back into my hands and frowned. He was a good kid, even though he spent his breaks getting high in the alley. "Are you feeling okay? Your face is bright red."

"I'm fine." Lyle's censure ended my musings, and for the next ten minutes, I focused on work. When Carter's order came up, I placed it on his table and kept my expression neutral. I was, after all, a grown woman capable of controlling her hormones. "Here you go."

"Thanks," he said, shifting back in his chair. The movement stretched his T-shirt tighter across his chest, outlining the roundness of his hard pecs, the line down his sternum, and the outline of a nipple ring. *A nipple ring.* Lordy. The flush returned to my cheeks. I fanned my face with a cardboard drink coaster from my apron pocket. Why did he have to be so fuck-hot? Bastard.

"No problem." But it *was* a problem, one I needed to get a grip on before I embarrassed myself. I tilted my nose to the ceiling, drew in a lungful of cinnamon- and coffee-scented air, and tried to center myself.

"Are you helping Rhett and Bronte move this weekend?"

Morning sunlight streamed through the window. The bright rays illuminated his irises and the flecks of gold in them, turning them to liquid amber. He reminded me of a lion, powerful and golden, with his sun-streaked brown hair spilling over his shoulders. I didn't like long hair on men, but he knew how to rock it like no one's business. In my fantasies, I dug my fingers into his hair and pulled until he growled.

"Um, no. I mean, yes." The question caught me off guard. Aside from forced pleasantries and the occasional inappropriate proposition, this was the closest we'd ever come to having a conversation. "You?"

"Yeah, Rhett suckered me into it." His index finger circled the rim of the espresso glass, drawing my attention to his thumb ring and the star tattoo right below it. "Crazy, isn't it? The two of them? I'd never have guessed."

"What's that supposed to mean?" My thoughts turned dark and mistrustful, as they always did with men. I narrowed my eyes and prepared to light his ass up. Was he digging at Bronte's disabilities, her OCD and autism? Family meant everything to me. No one—and I mean *no one*, no matter how hot—dissed my family. "She can't help the way she is."

"Don't get your panties in a twist. I'm Bronte's biggest fan. The girl is scary smart. I meant that I'm glad they met." His eyes widened. I bit my lower lip, knowing I was out of line but unable to help it. Something about him made my skin itchy hot on the inside, an itch that couldn't be scratched by simple conversation. He dropped a spoonful of sugar into the espresso and stirred, the silver clanging against the ceramic cup. "Bronte's one in a million. She's been good for him."

"They're good for each other." I searched his face for signs of insincerity but found none. My shoulders, which had been inching toward my ears, lowered a notch. "I never thought she'd find someone who understands her, but Rhett seems to be a good guy."

"He's the best." Placing his strong, capable hands flat on the table, he held my gaze. "I've known him all my life. When Amy died, I thought he'd never recover, but Bronte changed all that. I hope they're always as happy as they are now."

"Yeah, me too." Somehow, this womanizing pig had managed to voice my exact thoughts better than I could. My younger sister had always been career-driven, preferring the solitude of her laboratory to the company of men, while I'd been a serial dater since the age of fourteen. She'd hit the lottery with Rhett and found her bliss. After clearing my throat, I tapped a finger on the table, eager to escape his knowing eyes and oppressive maleness. "Well, enjoy your coffee. Let me know if you need anything else."

He jerked his chin in acknowledgement then turned his gaze to the window. With a sigh of relief, I cleared one of the tables, happy to be free of his spell. Unfortunately for me and my damp panties, instead of leaving after his drink, he stayed for another two hours and consumed enough espresso to give a normal person heart failure. I made Lyle refill his cup while I steered clear of him.

My eyes continued to drift in his direction, and the tension between my thighs continued to grow. After Harold had dumped me, I'd haunted nightclubs, picking up a guy here and there, but had carefully guarded my heart. No dates, no sleeping over, just sex. Because, well, *sex*. No one should go without it. Lately, I'd been too exhausted from work and caring for Dad to do more than crawl home at night and collapse into my bed. Being around Carter reminded me how long it had been and how much I missed a man's touch.

Catching my stare, Carter made a beeline toward me, a delicious, cocky smirk on his face. *Damn it.* I tried to push through the swinging doors into the kitchen, but Lyle was on his way out from the other side. I came up short, cursing under my breath, narrowly missing a black eye. Lyle brushed by with a brief apology. I smiled and stepped aside. *Just be cool. He'll be gone in a minute.* Instead of leaving though, Carter paused at the register and waited until I lifted my gaze to his.

"I was wondering if you might be free after work," he said, catching me off guard for a third time.

"Uh, what?" I dropped the empty tray I'd been holding. It clattered on the floor.

"I thought maybe we could grab a bite to eat or something."

Holy sweet baby Jesus. I gripped the counter with both hands, head spinning. "You mean, like a date?"

"No, like two people having a late lunch." His lips twitched. "Or we could hook up. I'm good with that too." Okay, there was the Carter I knew—crass, bold, and unapologetic. "Unless you have something else to do."

"Yes." I shook my head, clearing away the fog of pheromones. "I mean, yes, I have something to do."

"Maybe I could give you a lift home then?"

My car, a rusted and tired Chevy Cavalier, had finally given up, leaving me without transportation until I could save enough to fix it or buy something else. I hated riding the bus and couldn't afford taxi or Uber service. However, the thought of sitting in close confines with him might prove too much for my sex-starved ovaries. And what I needed to do after work required total secrecy. "It's okay. I wouldn't want to take you out of your way."

"It's not a problem."

Before I could protest, several things happened in rapid succession. The bell over the door rang. A familiar young man wearing jeans and a polo shirt stepped into the order line. Carter pushed me behind the cash register. Stunned into silence by his rough action, I gaped. The young man took one look at Carter, turned an impressive shade of gray, and sprinted toward the exit. Carter pounced. The two of them tumbled to the floor, rolling and grunting, overturning a table in the process, shattering the display of specialty muffins into a hundred pieces.

"Stop it!" I lunged toward Carter, slipping on the mess. "You're destroying my shop."

"Get back," Carter growled. He held me away with one hand while pressing a knee into the back of the struggling young man.

"What are you doing? Let him go." I shoved Carter's hand aside.

Seeing his chance for escape, the captive took advantage of Carter's distraction. He squirmed from beneath Carter's weight and crawled on all fours toward the door. Carter caught him by the ankle, but the guy had reached the threshold. Gripping the door frame with both hands, he levered himself onto the sidewalk, found his feet, and broke into a gallop across traffic. Carter rocketed out the door, hot on his trail, and disappeared between two taxis.

The couple at the table next to me scurried out the door, abandoning their untouched coffee. The rest of the patrons followed in rapid succession.

"Oh, no. Please." I scrambled after them. "Everything's fine now. They're gone. Please don't go." It was too late. The door banged shut behind the last customer, leaving me alone with Lyle and the mess on the floor. "Oh, no. No, no, no."

I gripped my head with both hands and debated if I should curse or cry. Business had been sketchy for the past few months. Even though I'd cut staff and expenses to the bone, we hadn't turned a profit in six months. The little bit of money I'd set aside for emergencies had dwindled down to pennies. With the arrival of a new national coffee franchise down the street, I couldn't afford this kind of bad publicity.

"Grab a broom and a trash can," I said to Lyle. Moping and whining would have to wait. "I'll get the mop."

The bell dinged over the door again. Hopeful, I turned to greet whoever it was. The smile slid from my face. Damn. It was the bastard. "No. Hell no." I pointed to the door. "Out. Out, out, out."

"Do you have any idea what you just did?" The amount of anger in his voice forced me back against the wall. His brows drew sharply together. He took a menacing step toward me, fingers clenched at his sides.

"Me? Are you kidding? Look what you did to my place." The

nerve of this guy. I accepted his challenge, closing the gap between us until we were less than a foot apart. I glared up at him. Geez, he was a lot bigger up close—all bulging muscle and teeming with testosterone. Even in my anger, I recognized the scent of his shampoo and body wash, fresh and outdoorsy, masculine and clean.

"I've been chasing that guy for months. If I don't bring him in, I'm out ten grand." He shoved a hand through his hair, temporarily distracting me from my anger. "Now I'm never going to catch him." A deep growl rumbled through his chest. "Fuck."

My heart skipped a beat. I was still pissed but oh so turned on by his show of temper. A guy with that amount of passion had to be a stallion in bed. I had a quick, inappropriate flash of him between my legs, directing that emotion into a more constructive activity. Sweat beaded on my temples. I glanced away, searching for anywhere to look but into his angry, delicious eyes. Then my gaze fell on the tumbled table, the broken chair, the spilled coffee and crushed muffins. My temper flared.

"I don't feel sorry for you. Look at this mess." I swept a hand around the empty room. "You destroyed my shop, drove away my customers. This place is a total disaster." Tears stung my eyes. I blinked them into submission and tried not to think about the mounting utility bills, payroll taxes, and the overdue rent. "Everyone left. They'll tell all their friends that Joe's Java Junction is full of crazy psychos. They'll never come back, and I wouldn't blame them." I poked an index finger into his chest. It was like poking an oak tree. "You— You're—" I sputtered, searching for something bad enough to call him. "You're a caveman."

"Is that the worst thing you can think of?" He grabbed my finger, wrapping it in his strong, calloused fingers. An electrical current coursed up my forearm into the tips of my breasts, tightening the nipples. His gaze fell to the offending body parts. They poked through the thin cotton of my T-shirt. I wanted to leap into his arms, wrap my legs around his waist, and yank on that long, glorious hair.

Horrified, I jerked my hand free and crossed my arms over my chest, but not before a smirk curled the corners of his mouth.

"Don't you dare laugh. It's not funny. Not at all. You have no idea what you've done." I shook my head and focused on the damage. My shoulders slumped in defeat. In my experience, this was what men did. They left a trail of brokenness in their wake, expecting the women to clean it up. "Just get away from me. Get out of my shop."

I left him in the middle of the room, went to retrieve the mop bucket, and prayed he'd have the common sense to leave. When I came back, he was still there, broom in one hand, dustpan in the other. I froze, certain this had to be a hallucination.

"Don't just stand there," he said, not looking at me. "Let's do this."

We worked together in silence. Tension stretched between us, so thick it made my lungs ache. I tried to ignore the swell of his biceps as he righted the table and the intoxicating scent of his cologne whenever he ventured too close. Thirty minutes later, the place looked tip-top, almost as good as new. The damage to my business, however, couldn't be repaired by soap and water.

I returned to my place behind the counter, preparing to close out the register.

He followed me and dropped a wad of money on the cash drawer. "For the damages."

I stared at the folded bills, stunned, before thumbing through them. A thousand dollars? "This is way too much," I protested, but he had already walked out the door.

CHAPTER 3
CARTER

I spent the rest of the day filling out paperwork and trying to forget Benson's escape by drinking at my favorite pub. The waitress gave me a smile as she placed a beer on the table. A few minutes earlier, she'd written her phone number on the palm of my hand.

I smiled back at her. "Thanks, babe." Across from me, Rhett rolled his eyes. I cocked my head. "Got something to say?"

"Nope." He tipped up his beer, meeting my glare with cool amusement.

"Go ahead. I can take it."

"You'll continue down your path of self-destruction no matter what I say. I'm not going to waste my breath." In all the years I'd known Rhett, he'd never censored his opinion, not once. His silence got my attention.

"Seriously?" I rested a forearm on the table and leaned forward. "Not one word? You don't want to lecture me about the dangers of promiscuity or the odds of getting an STI or the joys of monogamy?"

"Nope." He took another swallow of his beer.

"What if I told you that I screwed your mom's best friend at our high school graduation party?" I hadn't, but I knew it would get him going.

"Jesus, Carter." Rhett slammed a hand onto the table. The wall crumbled around his self-control. *Score.*

I chuckled, pleased with myself. Nothing gave me more pleasure than to ruffle Rhett's stringent code of honor. "No, not really, but see those two girls over there?" I nodded toward a pair of thirty-something brunettes at the bar who were casting doe eyes in my direction. "I did sleep with them."

"I don't want to know." He raised the palm of his hand in a show of surrender.

"Both of them. At the same time. A *ménage a trois* with lots of *ménage.*" I waggled my eyebrows, biting back laughter at his visible disgust.

"Jo was right. You're a pig."

"She talks about me?" My ears perked at the mention of my favorite barista, the two ladies instantly forgotten. Rhett shook his head and groaned in consternation. I twirled a finger in the air between us. "Come on. Talk. What else did she say?"

"Not much, except that you're disgusting." One corner of his mouth twitched with suppressed humor. He was enjoying this way too much, but I let him have his moment. It was what we did; we teased each other mercilessly.

"Does she mention me very often?"

Before I could ask more questions, the waitress returned with another mug of beer. "From the ladies at the bar." Her voice held a note of disapproval.

"Thanks, ladies." I raised the mug in a mock toast and ignored the waitress. They smiled and toasted back to me.

"Even after all these years, the size of your balls never fails to amaze me," Rhett said.

"It's not the size of my balls that they're after," I said, enjoying the way he rolled his eyes in pretend disgust. "But I don't do repeats. One and done. That's my motto. Or, in their case, two and done." As enjoyable as our little *ménage a trois* had been, a repeat would ruin the perfection of the encounter, risking hurt feelings and imagined emotional attachments. And everyone knew that I didn't do emotions or attachments or feelings.

"Don't you get tired of it? One-night stands? Living alone?" He shifted in his seat and slung an arm over the back of the booth.

"Don't you get tired of sleeping with the same woman every night?" His disapproval didn't bother me. Rhett believed in hearts and flowers and that happily-ever-after bullshit. Now that he was in love, he'd grown worse. Although he was a romantic sap, it didn't mean I liked him any less. In fact, I liked him more. His attitude gave balance to my warped and jaded outlook.

"Never." A grin brightened his features. "She's the best part of my day. You should try it sometime."

"Me? Hell no." I took a large swallow of beer to wash away the sour taste left in my mouth by the concept of monogamy. "Maybe when I'm ninety."

"When you're ninety, it won't matter. You'll be fat and bald. Those huge balls of yours will be dragging around your ankles, and you won't be able to get it up anymore."

"Probably." Aside from Rhett's friendship, I'd been alone most of my life and figured I'd go out of this world the same way. I pushed the notion aside, having accepted the idea years ago. "At least I'll have some kick-ass stories to tell your grandkids. I'll be crazy Uncle Carter, the one who's always drunk at Thanksgiving and pees in the potted plants." We shared a laugh, but something about the idea left queasiness in my gut.

"Hang on a sec." He lifted a finger then withdrew his phone from his pocket. The refrains of his ringtone, a sappy ballad, floated across our table. I groaned. Rhett narrowed his eyes in warning before turning his attention to the caller. "Hey, angel."

Okay, so maybe I was a little jealous of his relationship with Bronte. They held hands in public, stared at each other with starry eyes, and spoke in intimate, hushed tones, like they shared some precious secret. If I believed in the bullshit of love for even a second, I'd have to admit that he'd found his soulmate. Watching him now, the way his face lit up during their conversation, the laughter in his voice, it made me question everything I knew about women and relationships. And I hated questioning myself.

"Yeah, he's here," Rhett said into the phone. The hairs on the back of my neck lifted in warning. His gaze met mine, mischief dancing in the depths of his eyes. "Bronte wants to know if you'll pick up Jo tomorrow on the way to our place. The transmission went out of her car."

"No." I shook my head and drew a finger across my throat in a slitting motion.

"He said sure." Rhett smirked. "Love you, baby. See you in a bit."

"That was a dick move," I said once he'd ended the call.

"You're the dick. Her house is on your way. There's no reason you can't do it." He stared me down. "Give me one good reason, aside from the fact that you're an asshole."

"Uh, well, there was an incident." I glanced away, feeling a flood of guilt, then gave him the short version of the coffee shop fiasco. At the end of the story, he shook his head, and I tried to pretend like I hadn't fucked up. "What? Don't look at me that way. You know how long I've been tracking this dude. I've got ten thousand big ones riding on him, and I was a frog's hair away from catching him."

He lifted both hands into the air. "I didn't say anything."

"You didn't have to. It's written all over your face."

"What's ten thousand dollars to you? A week's vacation in Miami" He had a point, but I was too stubborn to concede. "A day of lost business for Jo could be the end of the coffee shop."

"I doubt that."

He leaned forward, lowering his voice. "She can barely make ends meet. Bronte and I have been trying to help, but we're not rich. If things don't turn around soon, they're going to have to close."

"I paid her for the damages, and I helped her clean up." Spoken aloud, the words sounded hollow. Now I really did feel like a dick. I could have waited for the guy to leave before tackling him, but I'd been consumed by the need to capture Clarence, overcome by the flood of adrenalin at the sight of my prey. I rubbed the spot on my chest where she'd poked me with a finger. "Okay, so I fucked up. It wasn't intentional. Either way, I'm the last person she wants to see."

"An even better reason for you to make amends." Rhett held his ground. "I need you two to get along. I'm going to marry Bronte sooner or later, and we'll all be family. It's important to me."

If he'd said anything else, I would have bailed, but I couldn't disappoint Rhett. Few people in the world mattered to me the way he did. "Fine. I'll do it, but if this goes wrong, I'm blaming you."

"She's maybe all of five-two and a hundred pounds. If she kicks your ass, you're going to have to turn in your man card." He chuckled. "Not that it wouldn't do you some good. I'd love to see a woman put you in your place."

The next day, a bizarre case of nervous anxiety hit about the same time I reached Jo's address. I parked the Escalade on the curb in front of an aged two-story house with faded paint and a bicycle leaning against the porch. I honked the horn. No response. I texted. No reply. After a couple of minutes, I strode up the sidewalk, grumbling under my breath. The scent of freshly cut grass permeated the late spring air. I knocked on the door then rubbed my sweating palms on the thighs of my jeans. An older guy answered the door.

"Is Jo here?" I asked, feeling eighteen years old and out of sorts.

"Who wants to know?" He looked me up and down, a curious gesture, considering he was the one wearing boxers and a T-shirt, and I was fully dressed.

"I'm Carter Eckhouse, Rhett's friend. I'm here to give Jo a ride to Bronte's." I extended a hand, and he took it in a warm, tight grasp.

"Nice to meet you, Carter. I'm the dad. You can call me Mr. H."

He turned away, leaving the door wide open, and trudged into the house. "Come on in." As we passed the stairway, he hollered, "Jo, your guy's here."

Bright light beamed through the slats of lowered blinds. I followed him down a neat but narrow hallway. Floral wallpaper covered the walls, the colors faded, the paper torn in spots. A grandfather clock ticked loudly from the first-floor landing of the staircase, and the sounds of a television drifted from the living room. The delicious aroma of baking meat hung in the air. Mr. H gestured to a dilapidated recliner next to the TV and sank into its twin. I hesitated. This was supposed to be a quick stop to get the girl, not a visit, and I was totally unprepared to deal with a parent.

"What's up with your hair?" He popped the footrest into the air and leaned back to study me. "In my experience, a man with hair like yours is either unemployed or a hippie. Are you a hippie?" He cocked an eyebrow.

"Not at all. I'll have you know, the ladies love this." I'd pulled my thick hair into a bun to keep it out of my eyes while I worked. By contrast, the smooth crown of Mr. Hollander's head reflected the blue light of the television. Tufts of reddish hair stuck out behind his ears. "Jealous?"

"Ha." He slapped his knee and hooted. "Hell yes, I'm jealous. I've been bald since I was thirty." The recliner groaned as he shifted his weight. "If you're not a hippie, you must be unemployed. You got a job, son?"

"I own a few businesses." At the lift of his eyebrows, I grinned. I respected his directness and his sense of humor. "All legitimate and quite profitable."

"Football or basketball?" His eyes narrowed.

"Basketball."

"Ever been in jail?"

I blinked at the rapid-fire questions. "More times than I can count. But the Marine Corps straightened me out."

"That so?" His blunt-tipped fingers scratched through the scruff on his chin. "Why'd you get out?"

"Honorably discharged, sir. I took a piece of shrapnel in the leg." Although it had been years, the injury still ached like a mother whenever it rained or I over-trained at the gym.

"Well, thank you for your service." His voice softened. "It takes a real man to fight for his country."

"Dad, leave the guy alone." Jo entered the room and stood between her father and the TV, hands on her hips. Out of respect for her father, I tried not to ogle the way her layered tank tops clung to the full curves of her breasts or her tiny waist, but damn—she looked good enough to eat.

"A father's got a right to know who his daughter is dating," Mr. Hollander grumbled.

"We're not dating," Jo and I said in unison.

"Right." Mr. Hollander picked up the remote control and flipped through the channels, seeming to shift into another dimension. "You kids have fun. Tell Rhett he owes me fifty bucks on that last baseball game, and give Bronte a hug for me."

"Okay." Jo leaned down to drop a kiss on her dad's bald head. "There's meatloaf and potatoes in the oven for lunch. Listen for the buzzer. Take it out and let it sit for ten minutes before you eat."

"Got it." He made a shooing motion with his free hand, eyes glued to the TV. "Now get out."

I followed Jo to the front porch. Beneath the stretchy fabric of her yoga pants, her bottom swung like two ripe melons. I adjusted myself and cursed Rhett for making me promise to leave her alone.

She stopped abruptly at the top step and glared at me. "Were you staring at my ass?"

"No." I shifted my gaze to a point over her shoulder, to the yard and street beyond it. "Okay, maybe."

"Unbelievable." Her weary sigh split the air. "Just so you know, this wasn't my idea. Bronte and Rhett insisted that I ride with you."

"I get it." I shoved my hands into my pockets and tried to pretend my feelings weren't a little hurt. Sure, I was a dick, but I wasn't that bad, was I? "Back at you, sweetheart."

"Here." From inside her bra, she withdrew two one-hundred-dollar bills and waved them beneath my nose. "You gave me too much money yesterday."

"Keep it," I said, moving past her and toward the Escalade. "For your trouble."

"I don't want it." Her footsteps pattered on the sidewalk behind me. I opened the passenger door for her. She stopped short of the curb and inspected the shiny black vehicle with narrowed her eyes. "This is yours? Did you steal it or something?"

"No, I didn't steal it. Why would you say that?" This time I didn't even try to hide my dismay. I scrubbed a hand over my face, rallying my patience and curbing my temper. "What kind of person do you think I am, anyway?"

Her gaze seared over me, starting at my man bun, lingering on my beard, skimming over my black T-shirt and camouflage pants. Something tightened in my groin. Plenty of girls had checked me out before, but Jo's scrutiny took the term to a new level. Not to be outdone, I returned the favor, and fuck me if I didn't like what I saw. Her black yoga pants molded to slim hips and solid thighs meant to wrap around a man's waist. And she was so tiny, like I could pick her up and put her in my pocket, like she needed a man to protect her from the assholes in the world. I scratched my head and backed up a step, bewildered by my thoughts.

"You're trouble with a capital T. The kind of guy who bounces from job to job and blows through women the same way." She pushed past me, climbed into the passenger seat, and stared straight ahead. The partial inaccuracy of her assessment wielded a second blow to my ego.

"Come on." I closed her door and climbed in my side. "I've got a job." In fact, I'd built an impressive business around bail bonding and bounty hunting. With fourteen offices in four different states, I'd become a respected member in the business. After I fastened the seatbelt, I turned to face her and summoned my most charming smile. "Admit it. Every woman likes a man who's a little rough around the edges."

"Not me." She crossed her arms over her chest. I studied the fullness of her lower lip and the white line where her teeth bit into it. Her creamy skin was bare of makeup, glowing and healthy. "Believe me, you're everything I don't like in a guy."

"So you're a lesbian." I started the car and eased into the street.

"Just because I find you repulsive doesn't mean I don't like men." Her brow scrunched. "And that's a horribly sexist remark."

I gave her a sideways glance. Everything about her posture suggested otherwise—arms crossed over her chest, legs pressed tightly together, nose in the air. "Okay, so you're straight but you don't like sex. I'm guessing it's been what, like, a year?"

She twisted in her seat, mouth agape. "I'm not discussing my sex life with you, you pig."

"Ah, so I'm right."

"Stop." She lifted a palm in the air. "In case you're too dense to figure it out, I don't like you. You're arrogant, condescending, and demeaning toward women." My fingers tightened around the steering wheel. Most people found me charming, if unconventional, and her steadfast dislike confused me. "The only reason I'm tolerating you is for Bronte's sake."

"Damn." I smirked, certain she was kidding, because she couldn't be oblivious to the sexual tension unfolding between us. One glance at her lowered brows proved me wrong. The smile slid from my face. I'd met some straight shooters in my day, but this girl won the prize. *I need you two to get along.* Rhett's words came back to me. I squared my shoulders and tried to remember my manners. "I apologize if I offended you."

"Maybe it would be best if we didn't talk," she said, training her attention outside the vehicle.

"Suit yourself." I followed her lead and focused on the road. The tension thickened between us. She smelled like cotton candy, sweet and tempting. I gripped the steering wheel tighter. Inside, I warred between anger and the desire to kiss her into submission. Most of the time, I didn't give a shit what anyone thought of me, but for some reason, her dislike offered the ultimate challenge. I was going to make her like me or die trying.

CHAPTER 4

JO

Rhett and Bronte had sublet a beautiful apartment in a historic building near the park. On the plus side, it was close to their work, had gorgeous hardwood floors, and a balcony overlooking the canal. On the negative side, the building had narrow stairways and no elevator.

"Tell me again why you didn't hire a moving service?" I asked Bronte.

We were stuck on the fourth-floor landing of the stairs with a sofa between us. Rhett and Bronte were on the lower side, while I was wedged between the sofa and handrail above the landing with Carter. No matter how hard we tried, we couldn't get the leather couch to navigate the ninety-degree angle to the next floor.

"Because we're trying to save a few bucks," Rhett answered for her.

I cringed inside. Despite my protests, they'd been helping with expenses for the coffee shop over the past couple of months. My best efforts at management had come up short. Business continued to decline, while our overhead skyrocketed. No one felt my failure more than me. Rhett's comment only increased my guilt. Although they were too polite to complain, I knew it was my fault.

"Try it again," Carter said. He was beside me, holding the bulk of the sofa's weight. When he shifted, the bulge of his bicep brushed my breast. Lust flooded my veins.

I closed my eyes against the sting of arousal. Everything about him irritated me, from his penetrating eyes to the woodsy scent of his cologne, and don't even get me started on his cocky smirk. To make matters worse, with each passing second in his presence, my panties grew damper.

"Lift it higher," he said. "Don't push so hard."

In my head, I could hear those terse commands given in the middle of a very intense, very erotic session of marathon screwing. My thighs wrapped around his waist. His hands on my ass. The two of us grinding and writhing and sweating. The walls of my sex shuddered. "Shit," I muttered.

"Jo, lift!" Rhett, Bronte, and Carter shouted in unison, jerking me out of my fantasy and back to the unpleasant reality of the staircase.

"I *am* lifting!"

"Okay, everyone, altogether. Now," Carter barked.

The four of us moved in unison, wedging the sofa tighter into the corner.

"This isn't working," Bronte said, her voice muffled by the piece of furniture between us. "The definition of insanity is doing the same thing over and over expecting different results. I think we're certifiable."

"I'll second that," Carter replied, his deep voice rumbling through the space between us.

"You need to lift it over the railing and angle it up," Bronte said.

"I think we should turn it on its side," Rhett added.

"My arms are starting to cramp." I'd been standing in the same position for at least ten minutes. Unlike Carter, my biceps weren't used to the heavy weight.

Carter shifted, taking more of the weight to lighten my load. In the process, he crowded me further into the railing. We were too close. The heat of his body shimmered over my side. The coarse hairs on his forearm tickled along my shoulder. The scent of his sweat and shower gel teased my nose. He was a dirty, sexy, wild man, and all I could think about was my thighs wrapped around his narrow hips while he rode me like a rodeo star.

"Mmmm." I hummed in approval, mesmerized by the thick vein running down his arm. I'd bet he could manhandle me just the way I liked it, moving me where he wanted, driving into me. Feeling the weight of his stare, I glanced up to find his predatory gaze on my face. I swallowed against the embarrassment thickening my throat. The corners of his eyes crinkled in amusement. Why did he have to be so damn delicious? He was a seven-course buffet of hotness, and I'd been on a diet for way too long.

"Don't even pretend like you weren't checking me out," he said.

"I wasn't."

"It's okay. Go ahead and look. I don't mind." His invitation sucked the stability out of my knees. I leaned against the railing for support. He chuckled. It was the first time we'd spoken directly to each other since the drive over.

"You're disgusting." I tilted my nose into the air. "Why do you have to be such a pervert all the time?"

He bent, his lips brushing over the shell of my ear, his words for me alone. "I get the feeling you like that about me."

"No." Yes, yes, *yes*. My sex quivered, and my earlobe burned where his lips had all but touched me. I turned my head, squeezing my eyes shut while I rallied my common sense. Being around him was pure hell. I had to get away, but I was trapped.

"Okay, let's try this again," Rhett said.

Carter lifted the sofa higher, giving me a great view of the way his T-shirt molded to his abs. I bit the inside of my cheek and fought the urge to run a hand down his chest. This time, I put my entire body weight into moving the sofa, eager to find escape. With one mighty coordinated shove from the four of us, the couch rounded the corner, and we managed to move it into the living room.

I retreated to the farthest corner of the apartment, as far away from Carter as I could get, and began unpacking boxes. Bronte fluttered between the rooms, her face pale. Lines of tension marred her freckled complexion. Although she was brilliant, she suffered from mild autism and Asperger's. Clutter and chaos disrupted her thought patterns, and I worried that the stress of moving might send her into a meltdown.

"No, no. This isn't right." She stared at the cluster of furniture near the dining room. "It's not balanced. There are too many chairs on that side. I can't breathe." Her chest rose and fell with a dozen short gasps. She rested a hand above her heart.

I dropped the armload of clothing in my arms, intending to rush to her side. Carter beat me there.

"How can I help?" he asked.

"Um, the table needs centered on the rug, and there should be six chairs, not five." Bronte bit her lower lip, glancing to me for reassurance. I nodded. "And I need a space to walk through the rooms. All this stuff, it's freaking me out."

Carter nudged the table to the left. "How's this?"

"No. That's too far. It needs to go up about three inches."

"Okay. What about now?" He worked with her for the next ten minutes. I held my breath, waiting for one of them to lose patience with the other. Carter continued to adjust the table. He never complained or grumbled. This patient, sympathetic side of his personality confused me. I watched and waited for him to break the façade, but he never did.

"Yes. Perfect." Bronte's shoulders lowered, and she let out a heavy sigh. "That's so much better."

"Great." The gold in his eyes shimmered. I wanted to press a kiss his full lower lip to express my gratitude. "I'll run down to the truck and find the other chair."

"I thought I could deal with this." Bronte waved a hand helplessly about the room but summoned a smile for Carter. "I'm being a pain in the ass. I'm sorry."

"Don't worry about it." A genuine smile transformed his sharp features into a thing of beauty. My pulse leaped. So the caveman could be charming when he wanted. Catching my expression, he winked as he headed toward the stairs. "I'll be right back. Try not to miss me."

"Not a problem," I replied haughtily, although the room seemed larger and emptier the second he crossed the threshold.

Rhett walked into the center of the living room. He'd been in the hallway, searching for Bronte's box of bathroom toiletries. One look at her, and a frown marred his forehead. "What do you need, angel?"

"Nothing. All good. Carter helped me," Bronte said. "I'll be fine once we get things put away. I'm just a little weirded out by the mess."

"Are you sure?" Rhett bent at the knees to catch her downturned gaze then glanced at me. I shook my head. Without exchanging words, he understood my concerns. Before he could say more, his phone buzzed with an incoming text. After a quick glance at the screen, he groaned. "Something's going on at the office. I need to run over there for a minute."

Bronte scowled at him. "You promised no interruptions today." I loved the way she spoke her mind to him, something she'd never been able to do with most people. He brought out the best in her, and I respected him for it.

"I know. I told them not to bother us, but this can't wait." He slipped an arm around her waist and pulled her to him. "It'll only take a minute. I promise."

They beamed at each other. He dropped a kiss on the tip of her nose. My heart squeezed at the depth of their connection. I valued her happiness above my own, but I couldn't help feeling a twinge of envy. Harold had been affectionate until our breakup, but he'd never looked at me the way Rhett looked at Bronte. My cheeks heating, I glanced out the window, feeling like a voyeur.

Carter returned with the missing chair. Our gazes collided, my emotions naked on my face. I broke the connection and pretended to dig for something in one of the boxes. I didn't like giving away my feelings, especially to a man. I focused on my concern for Bronte. "Why don't you go with him, sis? Grab some lunch while you're at it."

"I can't," she said, although her voice held a note of hopefulness. "There's too much to do here." Her shoulders began to rise again as she surveyed the apartment.

"It's okay," I said, giving them a smile. "Go ahead. Take your time. I'll keep working. I know how you like things. By the time you get back, I'll have the living room cleared, and you'll have a place to escape when the clutter gets overwhelming."

"Are you sure?" She glanced at Rhett then back to me, but the strain around her eyes melted. We smiled at each other.

"I'm sure. Go on." I flapped my hands in the direction of the door.

Thank you, Rhett mouthed over Bronte's head. With a protective arm around her shoulders, he ushered her toward the door.

Within seconds, they were gone. My selfless plan had one fatal flaw—now I was alone in the apartment with Carter. The silence amplified his breathing, thickened the air in the room, and intensified the ache of desire deep in my gut. I kept a wary eye on him. He seemed oblivious, focused on arranging the dining room table with meticulous care, verifying the distance between each chair with a measuring tape.

"Do you think this is okay?" he asked after he'd placed the final chair.

"Perfect."

At my praise, his face brightened with a smile. My heart doubled its cadence. I wanted to look away, but I couldn't, enchanted by the combination of sexiness and caring. Panic sliced through my chest. No man could be this patient, this giving. If he was, it would negate everything I'd come to believe, and I'd have to admit that not all men were douchebags. I needed to remember who he was, how much of an ass he could be.

I placed my hands on my hips. "Go ahead, say it. You know you want to."

"Um, you have giant tits?" He lifted an eyebrow, confusion reading plainly on his face.

And there he was, the asshole I'd come to know and despise. I huffed, feeling relief and a bizarre disappointment. "No. Bronte. She's weird. I know you're thinking it."

With a groan, he sank onto the edge of the sofa, like he'd finally run out of patience—not with Bronte, but with me. I waited for his temper to burst, for him to saunter out the door, but instead, he clasped his hands between his spread knees and shook his head. "Who am I to say what's weird and what's not? A little bit of crazy is what makes a person interesting. If you ask me, Bronte's more normal than me—or you."

I stared at him, unable to decipher the meaning behind his words. I was itching for a fight to ease the tension between us. "You don't have to stay. I'll catch the bus home when I'm finished."

He scratched his fingers over his chin, the good humor slipping from his face. "I don't mind."

"No, seriously. You can go." The longer we were alone, the weaker my resolve became. Every time he came within a yard of me, my nipples pebbled, and a funny twist happened in my lower belly. If we didn't get some distance between us, I was going to lick one of his smooth, bulging, sinful biceps, and that would be humiliating.

He slapped a hand on the box between us, making me jump. "What is your problem? I know you don't like me, but damn. At least I'm trying to get along."

If he had any idea how far he'd gotten beneath my skin, he'd laugh in my face. Maybe, if I made him angry enough, he'd go. "Is that why you keep staring at my ass and making pervy comments about my boobs?" I brushed his hand aside and opened the box, rummaging through the contents like a deranged squirrel.

"Jesus. Fine." He jumped to his feet and paced to the window. "No more sexual comments. I'll pretend like you're ugly. Is that what you want?"

"Yes. No." With a shaking hand, I swiped the hair out of my eyes. I had no idea what I wanted, except for the endless ache between my legs to stop.

"Fuck, you're impossible." At last, his temper snapped, but I felt no relief. Instead, the flash in his eyes lit a dozen tiny fires inside my womb. "I promised Rhett I'd make an effort to get along with you, but I didn't sign up for this kind of abuse."

He stalked toward me, brows lowered. The growl of his deep bass dissolved the bones in my knees. I placed a hand on the back of the sofa to hold myself up. He bent, close enough for me to feel the puff of his breath against my lips. And fuck me if it wasn't the hottest thing I'd ever experienced. I stared at his lips. *Kiss me, kiss me. Kiss. Me.* I spoke a silent prayer, begging him to put me out of my misery.

"You don't own Rhett and Bronte. Rhett's more family to me than my blood relatives. I'm here to help them. It doesn't have anything to do with you. If you don't like it, then you can leave, but I'm not going anywhere." He glared at me, an infuriating mix of male righteousness and smug self-conviction. "What do you have to say about that, Ms. Hollander?"

"Suit yourself." Unable to tolerate the intensity of his stare for one more second, I shoved the heavy box toward the bedroom. My stomach churned. I didn't like being mean. It went against my sunny nature. Now, having vented a bit of my frustration, I forced an apologetic smile. "I'm sorry. You've been nothing but helpful today, and I'm being a total bitch. Truce?" I extended a hand to shake.

He crossed his arms over his chest and stared at me. I was about to withdraw it and slink away in humiliation when he engulfed my fingers in his large hand. The warm roughness of his palm sent a shockwave of heat up my arm. We both froze. He dropped my hand like he'd been stung and shoved it in his pocket. His touch reverberated down to my toes.

"Truce then," he said in a voice so soft, I barely heard it.

"Okay. Well, let's get to it." Gathering my stunned wits, I tried to remember where I was and why. The stack of boxes and scattered furniture brought me back to reality. There was work to be done, and it wasn't going to do itself.

"What can I do?" Carter avoided my gaze, acting as stunned as I was.

"These boxes need to go to the bedroom."

"Which boxes?"

"The ones that say 'bedroom.'" After turning my back to him, I bent over to pick up another box. My backside burned with the weight of his gaze. "Carter! Seriously. Are you looking at my ass again? You promised."

"It's hard not to when you've got it stuck up in the air like that." His smirk was completely devoid of guilt. He laughed, the sound boyish and utterly charming. Damn it. We were back to that again—his hotness and my unrelenting crush.

I smiled, surrendering to his charm, and threw my hands into the air. "You're such a creeper."

"I know. I know. It's a gift." The shrug of his broad shoulders drew my eyes to their width. He was so solid and strong. "Here. Let me get it." Before I could protest, he heaved the box into his arms. His swollen biceps taunted me. Why, why, why did he have to be so hot? "Where does it go?"

"The walk-in closet." I pointed to the master bedroom.

"Can you get the door?"

I trotted in front of him, opened the closet door, and followed him inside. To my sister's credit, she'd found an apartment with amazing closet space. Built-in shelves and racks lined the walls. The door swung shut behind us, closing on silent hinges. "You can set it there, in the corner."

"Geez, this thing weighs a ton. What the hell is in here? Rocks?" He placed the box in the corners and straightened, flexing his arms, twitching his muscles like a bodybuilder.

Less than a foot separated us. Although the closet was larger than my bedroom at home, Carter's presence dwarfed the space. I swallowed, avoiding his gaze, trying to look anywhere but at him. The walls closed in on us until it was just him and me. Carter's eyes dipped to my lips and stayed there for one, two, three heartbeats. *Oh, Lord. Breathe, Jo, breathe.* Needing to escape his penetrating stare, I fled to the door. I turned the doorknob. Nothing happened. I rattled the handle and tried not to panic. "Shit. It's locked."

"No way. Let me try." In an instant, he was at my side, his large arm brushing against mine. "It's just stuck." One shove of his shoulder popped the door open. "Chill out."

"Why are you laughing? It's not funny." I drew in a deep breath and tried to calm the anxiety. "Closed spaces gave me the creeps."

Carter stared at me. Electricity crackled between us. His gaze flickered to my lips. "Are you always this tense?"

"I'm not tense." Turning my back, I fled to the living room. Carter followed me in silence. He moved the boxes to the appropriate rooms while I unpacked the books for the living room shelves. My gaze kept drifting back to him, his broad shoulders, narrow hips, and strong legs. When he returned to the room, I yanked my attention back to the task and tried to ignore the flush of heat in my cheeks.

"You and Bronte seem pretty tight," he said when all the boxes had been relocated. I paused to wipe the sweat from my forehead. He took a seat on the coffee table and rested his forearms on his thighs, clasping his hands between them. "Have you always been close?"

"Yeah, I guess." As her older sister, my job had always been to help and protect her. During our childhood, the neighborhood kids had bullied her. I'd been the one to wipe away her tears and hold her hand. "You don't have any siblings?"

"Not exactly." I quirked an eyebrow at his odd answer, but he quickly moved on to another topic. "Your dad's a character."

"Yeah." I smiled. "I wish you could've met him before Mom passed. He was something else." Dad had been a shadow of his former self since the funeral. Seeing him so broken hurt my heart.

"You were nice to him today. I haven't heard him laugh in a long time."

"You must really think I'm a dick." The heavy note of disappointment in his voice resurrected my guilt.

I rubbed my sternum, seeking relief that never came. "You have to admit that you can be a bit...abrasive sometimes."

His burst of heartfelt laughter brought the heat to my cheeks again. "I've been told that a time or two. Tell me, Jo, do you always say exactly what you're thinking?"

"Well, yes. Why wouldn't I?" Confused, I dropped my eyelids and peered at him through the veil of lashes. "I don't have time for bullshit."

"Yeah, neither do I. That's one thing we have in common." His gaze darkened, quickening my pulse. "I think we could be friends if we tried. You know, for Rhett and Bronte's sake. We could go out for drinks, have a little fun."

"Fun?" The word tasted foreign on my tongue. I used to have fun, before Mom died and Dad sank into depression. I'd had a fiancé and a job and my own place. There had been laughter and sunshine and playfulness. Those days seemed like a lifetime ago. "I don't have fun. Not anymore."

"Lucky for you, I'm an expert at it." The promise in his voice tickled my tummy. His eyes, usually clear and light brown, were dark and unreadable. "Having fun is one of my specialties."

"There's no time. I have Dad and Bronte and the coffee shop." Misery bubbled beneath the surface of my words. If he only knew how much I longed to throw aside my responsibilities and have an adventure.

"It happens that we both have an hour or so to kill." The bow of his lips arched further upward, taunting me. "We could take the edge off all those nerves you're fraying. No one will know. It can be our little secret." His gaze dipped to my mouth again. I felt my resolve melting away. *No one will know. No one will know.* If he had any idea how close I was to stripping off my clothes and dry humping his thigh, he wouldn't talk like that.

"My nerves aren't frayed." I ran the tip of my tongue over the parched roof my mouth, trying to gather the last remaining threads of my self-control.

"Whatever. Keep telling yourself that. Sometimes a good fuck can do wonders for a person's attitude."

I pressed my thighs together against the ache between them. "I don't know what kind of friends you have, but I don't have sex with mine."

"Well, you should. If you can't fuck your friends, who can you fuck, right?"

In spite of my best efforts, a giggle slipped out. "You're so messed up."

His eyes sparkled. I liked this playful, teasing Carter. "Come on, Jo. You've thought about it, right? You. Me. Pounding the sheets."

"No," I said, fighting against the flood of heat into my face at the lie. Lately, he'd been the star of every one of my late-night fantasies.

"I've thought about you. More than once." My eyes met his. He stared back, pupils dilated, lips parted. "I've wondered about those beautiful boobs, how they'd taste in my mouth. If your nipples are pink or brown. Do they pucker up like tiny rosebuds, or do they get hard and big and stick out like thimbles?"

I crossed my arms over my chest to hide the proof that they were small like rosebuds. No matter how hard I tried, I couldn't look away from his face. "You can't say things like that." But I liked it. I liked knowing that he thought about me in the privacy of his bedroom. "What else do you think about?"

His grin widened. "I wonder what kind of panties you're wearing. White cotton, lace and satin, boy shorts, or a thong? What's your favorite?"

"Thong." The word cracked in my dry throat. I ran the tip of my tongue over my lips to moisten them. "I like thongs."

"Me too." He shifted, running his palms along the length of his thighs. The movement stretched the fabric of his pants, outlining his dick—his long, hard, thick cock. Knowing that he was turned on by the conversation lessened my hesitance and snapped the last remaining shred of my self-restraint.

"I think about your chest." Emboldened by the fire in his gaze, I plunged headlong into the game. "If you shave it or if you've got hair there. How it would feel to run my fingers over it."

"You can see for yourself." In one fluid motion, he dragged his T-shirt over his head.

I bit my bottom lip to hold back a groan of appreciation. His pectoral muscles, smooth and tanned, twitched under my gaze. A gold ring pierced the left nipple. Ripples of muscle cascaded down his abdomen. Every inch of his torso was taut and lean and begging to be touched.

"Your turn." His gaze dipped to my cleavage.

Was I crazy for wanting to show him more? I fingered the hem of my top, wavering between lust and common sense. If I breached the barrier of distance between us, there'd be no going back. On the other hand, I longed to be wild and free, if only for one hour. Who better to do it with than the wildest guy I'd ever met? I lifted the hem of my shirt, baring the satiny cups of my bra.

A sudden pounding on the apartment door made us both jump. "Jo, are you in there?" Bronte called through the door. "We forgot our key."

Embarrassment flooded my cheeks. "Uh, yes." I yanked my shirt down and glared at Carter. What was I thinking? A few more minutes, and I would have thrown myself at him. He lifted an eyebrow and shrugged, a huge smile bowing his lips. I wanted to be mad at him, but I couldn't. He was just too darn hot. I shook my head and returned his grin.

"Hang on." Carter nudged me aside. He chucked me under the chin, his words quiet and only for me. "I like it when you smile. You should do it more often."

CHAPTER 5
CARTER

Once Rhett and Bronte were settled, I drove Jo back to her house. With every mile closer to home, she grew quieter and smaller, until we traveled in silence. I parked the car in the driveway. Her somber mood unnerved me. While she gathered her things, I went around to her side of the vehicle and opened the door. Then, like a good boy, I walked her to the front steps.

"I really wish you wouldn't do stuff like this," she said when we reached the front porch, her voice teeming with exasperation.

"What?" I shoved my hands into my pockets and rocked back on my heels.

"Where is my key?" She rummaged through the depths of her purse. "Be nice. Open my doors. Walk me to the house. It's confusing."

"You'd rather I was a dick? I thought we were past that."

"I don't know." She let out a sigh of relief. I didn't know if it was because she'd found the key or because she was finally going to be rid of me. "Here it is."

I took the key from her and stuck it in the lock. "I meant what I said earlier. I want us to be friends. It's the best thing for all of us."

"I believe your exact words were, 'if you can't fuck your friends, who can you fuck?'"

"Yeah. I did say that, but I didn't mean it." I rubbed the back of my neck sheepishly. "Not that I wouldn't love to fuck you, because I would, but I promised Rhett to stay out of your pants. And I've never broken a promise to him. Not yet."

"Carter, stop talking. You're making it worse." She studied me, her blue eyes delving deeper into my soul than I cared to reveal. I blinked away, uncomfortable, afraid she'd see the real me, the coward, the bastard, the kid no one wanted. "You know that guy at the coffee shop? Clarence? The one you jumped? You should have told me you were looking for him." She pushed open the door, leaving me at the doorstep with my mouth open. "I see him around all the time. He hangs out near my ex-boyfriend's apartment."

I groaned and hung my head. "Seriously?"

"Yeah, sure." She dropped her keys on a small table in the foyer and turned to face me. "I can give you the address."

"Yes!" I fist-pumped the air. In a flash, I resumed the thrill of the chase. This could be the break I'd been waiting for. "Don't yank my chain, Hollander. Are you sure it's the same guy?"

"One hundred percent."

"Come here." I grabbed her, bent her over backward until her feet left the ground, and kissed her. Not just any kiss, but long, deep, and lingering. Her fingers curled into my biceps, the nails cutting into the muscle. My tongue found hers. The soft, wet heat of her mouth erased thoughts of Clarence Mortimer Benson III and replaced them with desire. She leaned into me. I slid my hands down her ribs and grabbed a handful of her bottom. The press of her pussy against my groin made me instantly hard. *Shit.* What was I doing? I'd promised Rhett to stay out of Jo's bed. If I didn't stop now, we'd be fucking on the sidewalk in about ten seconds.

"That you, Jo?" Mr. H called from the darkness inside the house.

Reluctantly, I set her back onto her feet. Her lips were swollen and pink. She touched a hand to her mouth. Our ragged breathing broke the nighttime stillness. I adjusted the raging hard-on behind my zipper and gave her a lopsided smile.

"Yeah, Dad. It's me and Carter." Her eyes locked with mine, wild and wide, the pupils enlarged to black pools.

"You gonna invite him in, or are you gonna keep making out on the front porch?"

Jo rolled her eyes but smiled. I glanced down at the tent in my pants and shook my head. Her eyebrows lifted. "No. He can't stay."

"Good call," I said. I wrapped an arm around her waist and pulled her to me. Those big, luscious tits flattened against my chest. "I'll catch you later. If I get this guy, I'll pay you a finder's fee." I dropped one more kiss on her mouth then gave her a slap on the ass for good measure. A startled squeak punctuated her gasp. I turned and sauntered down the sidewalk under a sky bright with stars. "Night, Mr. H."

CHAPTER 6

JO

The screen door banged shut behind Carter as he left. I floated into the house on weak legs and a cloud of confusion. My lips throbbed, and the tips of my breasts tingled in the best way. I avoided the living room and headed straight for the stairs. I needed to process in my bedroom what had just happened, away from the prying eyes of Dad.

"Everything go okay?" To my dismay, Dad's voice boomed into the hallway before my foot hit the first step. "How is Bronte handling the change?"

With a sigh, I reversed direction and tried to rearrange my features into their normal nonchalance. The blue light of the television illuminated the room. As always, I found comfort in the dilapidated sofa, Mom's weathered armchair, and the faded throw rugs on the worn wood floor. Dad sat in front of the TV, a beer at his elbow and the remote control in his hand. He smiled at me through the darkness.

"She's doing well." I dropped a kiss on the top of his head. "You should visit. She'd love it."

"I don't know." He turned his attention back to the shopping channel, where a lady with too much makeup pitched the virtues of hair restoration serum. "We'll see."

"It wouldn't hurt you to get out now and then." I placed a loving hand on his arm. "Fresh air will do wonders. And I could use your help at the shop."

He stiffened beneath my touch. Since Mom had passed away at the coffeehouse, his visits had been minimal, him finding the place overflowing with her memories. "Maybe." The tone of his voice signaled the end of our conversation.

"Okay. Well, good night." Pushing away the disappointment, I squeezed his shoulder gently. "Don't stay up too late."

"Love you," he mumbled and covered my hand with his.

The stairs creaked as I headed to my room, reminding me of all the times I'd sneaked out of the house and returned in secrecy, only to be caught by the telltale steps. The memory gave me comfort, and after a quick shower, I flopped on the bed. Sleep eluded me. I replayed Carter's kiss over and over in my head. My toes curled, my lips still buzzing from his mouth on mine. He wasn't the kind of guy for a relationship, but if his kiss was any indication, he knew his way around a woman's body. I cupped my breast, feeling the rush of blood into the tip, the ache of arousal. Maybe I could push aside my boycott of men for a one-night stand with him. I fell asleep with my hand in my panties and a smile on my lips.

The ringtone of my phone woke me at three forty-five in the morning. Adrenalin yanked me into full consciousness. Although the number was foreign, I accepted the call, certain the world was ending.

"Hello? What's wrong?" My pulse thundered in my ears as my mind raced through worst-case scenarios. I wedged the phone between my neck and shoulder and jammed my legs into a pair of sweats. "Is it the coffee shop? Has someone had an accident?"

"It's me. Carter." His deep voice vibrated through the phone into my ear, tickling the nerve endings. "Don't panic. Nothing's wrong."

I froze, disbelieving. "Is this some kind of joke? Do you have any idea what time it is?" Although I tried to sound annoyed, I was secretly thrilled and savored the sound of his voice, warm and intimate, roughened by the early hour.

"I caught him." His excitement transferred through the airwaves. "I went straight to the address you gave me, knocked on the door, and the motherfucker answered."

"Really?" Tucking a foot beneath me, I settled against the pillows and smiled at his enthusiasm. "I'm glad it worked out."

"Yeah. Like I said, I've been chasing this guy forever. He's sitting in the Laurel County lockup as we speak. And I've got a big fat finder's fee for you."

"Oh, no. You don't have to pay me anything." Although I needed the money, my pride wouldn't accept it. I hadn't helped him in hopes of payment. My only motivation was to ease the tension between us. A second thought tempered my happiness for him. Now that he'd caught Clarence, he wouldn't be visiting the coffee shop anymore. The alarm clock blared from the nightstand. I slapped a hand over the shutoff and groaned. "I need to go. I've got to get to work."

"Shit. You get up this early every morning?"

I heard the rustle of fabric, like he was undressing, the sound of heavy boots hitting the floor, the jingle of coins on a dresser. Closing my eyes, I pictured his bare, muscular chest, the nipple ring, and the delectable cut of muscle below each hip bone. I swallowed and tried to push the thought out of my mind. "Every day, rain or shine. Like my dad says, that coffee's not going to make itself."

"Okay, well, I just wanted to call and thank you." His tone lowered, and I heard the higher pitch of a female voice in the background. I clenched my jaw. "You have a nice day, Jo Hollander."

"Thanks, Carter. You too." I ended the call and sank to the edge of the bed, feeling dejected, every muscle in my body aching with exhaustion. That should have been me in his bed. I didn't know who she was, but I begrudged her every touch of his fingers, every kiss of his lips. Then, I remembered Harold and the way he'd broken my heart. Because that was what men did. They lured you into their lair with kindness and false promises, and when they were done with you, they tossed you aside like you never mattered.

CHAPTER 7

CARTER

A few days later, I stopped by the coffee shop to give Jo the reward. One thousand dollars in cash might come in handy for her. A line of people snaked down the sidewalk and curled around the corner. I pushed my way to the front and inside to find Jo sweating behind the counter. At the first opportunity, I caught her gaze. She jerked her chin at me. A worried frown puckered her forehead.

"I can't talk. Lyle called off today." She had one hand in the muffin display and the other hand on the espresso machine. "Grab a seat. I'll call you when your order is done."

"Can I help?" I had no idea how to serve coffee, but the panic on her face was enough to make me want to try.

She tossed an apron at me. "Do you know how to run a cash register?"

After a quick tutorial, I took orders and rang them up while Jo made the coffee. I gained a new appreciation for how hard she worked. No matter how crabby the customers, she filled their orders with a pleasant smile. When the last customer had been served, I followed her through the swinging doors and into the back room. She hopped onto one of the counters and blew out a heavy sigh.

"My feet are killing me." As she spoke, she kicked off her sandals. Crossing an ankle over her knee, she kneaded the sole of her foot and winced.

"Where did all those people come from?" Brushing her hand aside, I took her small foot in my grasp and dug my thumbs into her arch.

"It's overflow from the art gallery. They're having a street fair today. I hoped to get a few of their patrons, but I had no idea it would be this crazy. You really helped. I'm not sure what I would have done if you hadn't show up when you did." Her head tipped back, eyes closing. A delicious moan accompanied each stroke of my fingers. I kept massaging, rewarded by her tiny grunts of ecstasy.

"No problem." Something funny happened low in my gut, something more than primitive lust. I cleared my throat and gently lowered her foot. "I just dropped by to give you this." I withdrew an envelope from my pocket and handed it to her.

"Like I said, it's not necessary." She waved my hand away, but her eyes remained trained on the envelope. "After what you did today, I couldn't possibly accept it."

"Don't argue. Just take it."

This time, she obeyed. She folded up the envelope and slipped it into her jeans pocket. "Thanks." I could still taste the sweetness of her mouth from our kiss the other night. She cleared her throat. "You never got your coffee today. I could make some for you. On the house."

"No." The last thing on my mind was coffee. I wanted to take her in my arms and do dirty things to her hot, tight little body—my cue to leave. "I probably should get out of here."

"Yeah, probably." Her gaze dipped to my mouth then crawled back to my eyes.

I knew that look. I'd seen it in other girls. She wanted me. The feeling was mutual. If she'd been anyone else, if I hadn't promised

Rhett, I'd have thrown her against the wall and fucked her until we both saw stars. Instead, I ran a hand through my hair and backed away. "Well, I'd better let you get back to work."

Back at the office, I propped my feet on the desk and stared at the computer screen with unseeing eyes. Life had taken an unexpected turn for the better, beginning with the capture of Benson. Spending the morning with Jo had put the icing on the cake. She was one hell of a girl. I respected her work ethic and the way she shouldered so much responsibility without complaint. The more I knew of her, the more I liked her.

"You're looking awfully smug today." Darcy entered my office and dropped a pile of paperwork in the center of the desk. Her dangling earrings jingled with each toss of her hair.

"It's a beautiful day." Jo had sent a plate of oatmeal chocolate chip cookies home with me. I took one and shoved the entire thing into my mouth. It melted on my tongue in a combination of textures, rough oatmeal and smooth chocolate. Like Jo, it was soft and sweet and mouthwatering.

Darcy's eyes narrowed. "For you, it's a great day. For me, not so much. I was looking forward to a new Mercedes." She cocked a hip and rested a hand on it, challenging me with her gaze.

"Ah, right. Jo scooped up your bonus, didn't she? I guess maybe next time you'll be a little bit quicker." I decided to let her stew for a bit. Unbeknownst to her, the Mercedes was on order and set to deliver in a few weeks. I rewarded my employees for their hard work. She might have missed the mark on Benson, but she'd been instrumental in making my business a success.

"Who is this girl, anyway?" She plopped into one of the leather club chairs across from my desk and helped herself to a cookie. Her yellow-and-green plaid skinny jeans warred with the calm gray tones of my office. As the president of the company, I refused to enact a dress code. In my opinion, a person should wear what made them feel good, and if bright, obnoxious colors lifted her spirits, I was all in.

"She's Bronte's sister—you know, Rhett's girlfriend? Her family owns Joe's Java Junction, the coffee shop down by the college." The high-backed leather chair squeaked as I crossed my legs at the ankles.

Darcy followed suit, crossing her legs and resting her shoes on the opposite corner. "Yeah? Never been there. I might have to go check her—the coffee shop—out." Her sharp gaze roved over me.

"She's something else. You'd like her." Unable to restrain my grin, I beamed and handed her another cookie.

"You certainly seem smitten." She nibbled the edges, peering over the top like a curious mouse.

"Hardly. We're friends." In all of my twenty-nine years, I'd never had a female friend. This was a huge deal for me. I shoved aside the thought before I panicked.

"So she's ugly." A smartass smirk curved Darcy's bright pink mouth.

"That's a hateful thing to say." With the tip of my boot, I knocked her feet off the desk. "Sounds like someone is jealous."

"You wish you had something this good." Darcy waggled her thin, penciled eyebrows. With a fifteen-year age gap between us, she was more like a mother to me than my actual mom. We'd been through a lot together. Aside from Rhett, she was my most trusted friend.

I opened my mouth to reply but was cut short by the sight of my sister, Reagan, entering the reception area. "Shit." My feet hit the floor with a thud. I straightened in the chair and brushed cookie crumbs from the front of my T-shirt.

Darcy's gaze followed mine. "Oh, yeah, I forgot. Your sister is coming by this afternoon."

"Seriously, Darcy? A little warning might have been nice." With less than three months separating our ages, my half-sister and I enjoyed a unique dynamic. We were joined by blood, separated by secrets, and united against our father's dictatorship.

Reagan strode directly into my office. Although we shared the same paternity, she resembled her mother in coloring—her eyes a cool, misty blue, like a turbulent ocean, her skin lighter and more translucent. "Carter, you're here. Great. We need to talk. Hi, Darcy."

"Hey, doll." Darcy stood and air-kissed Reagan on the cheek. "You look fabulous today."

"Thanks. Oh, I love your shoes. I wish I could wear something like this, but my stylist would have a fit." Reagan held Darcy at arm's length to admire her outrageous outfit. Darcy preened, pointing the toes of her fire-engine-red platform pumps. Reagan, by contrast, wore an expensive cream pantsuit and taupe flats, the picture of classic conservatism.

"Thanks." The two women beamed at each other.

I cleared my throat. If I didn't interrupt, their love fest would last another hour.

"Don't start." Reagan lifted a manicured finger into the air, expression stern. Her shiny hair, the same shade of brown as mine, swirled around her shoulders in perfect waves. "I need to know if you're coming to the wedding. I haven't gotten your RSVP yet."

"You know I can't go."

"Yes, you can. You're my brother, and I want you there."

I stared at her, certain I'd misheard. Our relationship was a secret. No one knew that we'd found each other through an absurd twist of fate, especially our father. If he knew, he'd have a shit fit. Although I relished the thought of causing him distress, I didn't want to cause problems for my mother. Even if I wanted to go, I couldn't risk hurting her. "No."

"Come on. You didn't even think about it." Her tone turned wheedling, like she was fifteen instead of thirty. I wished that I'd known her then, that our childhood hadn't been stolen from us.

"I don't have to think about it. I'm not going to rub shoulders with two hundred strangers—"

"Five hundred," she interjected.

"—five hundred strangers in a monkey suit just to watch you marry a guy with a spray tan."

"First of all, he doesn't spray tan. He's half Italian and naturally dark. Second, I need you there for moral support. You're the only one who understands the way Daddy can be." She smiled brightly, unfazed by the rejection, and rested a hip on the corner of my desk. The afternoon light brought out the gold in her eyes, eyes shaped like mine. "Besides, you know it'll piss Daddy off. That should be reason enough for you." Her soft, pale hand covered the back of my rough, tanned one. "You can sit in the back if you're worried about what people will think. I just want you to be there."

"It doesn't worry me. I don't give a shit about what your society crowd thinks," I said gruffly. "It's the whole marriage thing. It gives me the creeps." The concept of committing to one woman for all eternity sent a shiver down my back. "Besides, the church will probably burn down if I step inside."

"Nonsense. The angels will sing in glory." She lifted her hands to the sky, mocking me with a playful grin. "It might do you good. Your soul could do with a little saving."

"It means that much to you?" Deep down, we both knew I'd give into her request but not without a fight. "And what about Senator Mayfield? Does he know that you invited me?"

"Daddy doesn't call all the shots." Mischief twinkled in her eyes. "At least not after I marry Davis. Come on. Don't make me beg."

"I'll go to the wedding, but not the reception." The elation on her face provided a bigger reward than any bounty.

"You'll go to both." With two fingers, Reagan lifted the small sculpture acting as a paperweight on my desk. "What is this?"

At first glance, the statue appeared to be a modern interpretation of two intertwining trees. I took it from her and turned it upside down. From this vantage point, the sculpture morphed into a round woman giving a blow job to a tall, spindly man. Reagan's mouth formed a horrified O. I smirked.

"That's disgusting." She rolled her eyes.

"I like it." I replaced the statue next to the stapler and folded my hands on the desktop.

"Back to the topic." She stood and smoothed her jacket. "You're going to do this for me, Carter. You're the only brother I have." Her eyes flashed with the passion of her words. We hadn't known each for very long, but I could see so much of my father in the clean lines of her face. Thank goodness she'd inherited his good qualities and not the bad. "I want all my family around me."

"Fine. I'll go." Why did I cave? Maybe I wanted to be normal, to have a family, to feel like I belonged somewhere to someone—anyone. Reagan was the only relative who gave a shit about me, and I couldn't bear the idea of disappointing her.

"Yes! Yay!" She grabbed my face and smacked a kiss on my forehead. "I knew I could count on you."

"You're going to owe me for this. Big time," I grumbled, in mock irritation.

"Sure. Whatever you want." The radiant happiness in her smile mitigated my misgivings. "And please bring a date."

"Whoa. That's just crazy talk." I shook my head. "No date."

"Don't argue with me, Carter. It's my day, and you've got to do what I say. If you go stag, it'll make the guest count uneven at your table. Besides, I don't want you hitting on the other bridesmaids or the guests."

"Do you seriously think I'd do something like that?"

"In the year that I've known you, you've slept with my housekeeper and my psychiatrist. I trust you with my life, but I don't trust you to keep your penis in your pants."

I chuckled.

Reagan, however, missed the humor in the situation. She slapped a palm on the desk, making the paperclips jump. "This is serious, Carter. It's bad enough that I'm marrying a man I hardly know so Daddy can run for Vice President. If I have to put up with all this political bullshit, I want this wedding to be perfect. No shenanigans."

"Geesh. Okay." To show my surrender, I lifted my palms into the air. "Chill out, bridezilla."

"And get a haircut." Although steel edged her tone and words, a smile lurked in her eyes.

"No. Absolutely not." As much as I loved her, I had to draw the line somewhere. I'd been growing my hair for the past three years. "It's my strength. And the chicks dig it."

"Carter, Carter, Carter." Reagan tsked and shook her head. "What kind of decent girl is going to go for a guy who looks like a deranged mountain man?" Her gaze dropped to the tattoo above the base of my thumb, the thickness of my beard, the length of my hair.

"I don't need any help with the ladies," I said. The direction of the conversation left an uneasy feeling in the pit of my stomach, one I'd have to analyze some other time.

"When I said bring a date, I meant a *respectable* girl. None of your barroom floozies." She glared at me, her expression identical to mine. We might have different mothers, but we definitely came from the same father.

"Give me a break." Even as I complained, I recognized the truth in her statement. "Darcy can come with me."

"Oh, no." Darcy waved her hands through the air, plastic bracelets jangling. "I have a husband, and he doesn't share. You're on your own, mountain man."

"You have a few weeks to figure it out." Reagan shouldered the strap of her large, expensive designer bag before giving my face a short, playful slap. "Darcy, make sure he gets a tuxedo, will you? I don't have time to babysit him. Now, I've got to meet the florist. There's a problem with the flowers. Walk me to the car, Carter."

When we reached the pristine white Audi on the opposite side of the street, I opened the car door for her. She gave me a smile and a kiss on the cheek before driving away. I watched the car until it disappeared into midday traffic. I dragged a hand over my jaw, fingers stroking through my beard. This wedding had disaster written all over it. Lucky for Reagan, I enjoyed stirring up trouble.

CHAPTER 8

JO

A few days passed. Carter stayed in my thoughts. Mostly because he kept showing up at the coffee shop every morning. I tried to avoid him, but it was impossible to ignore his lion eyes. They followed me around as I worked. I found myself gravitating to his table just to hear his rumbling voice. With great effort, I managed to be civil, not too friendly but aloof. This crazy crush of mine had to end. Anything more than friendship with Carter was destined to end in disaster.

Who was I kidding? I didn't want a man at all. Harold had destroyed my self-confidence and my heart in one fell swoop. He'd been kind, generous, and adoring right up until the moment he'd become cold, cruel, and heartless. In the beginning, everything had been perfect. Although his work had forced him to commute between Laurel Falls and Chicago, we'd found a way to spend time together. Eventually, we'd moved into an apartment. One day, I'd come home to find his demeanor changed and my bags packed. He didn't love me anymore. We were over.

"I'll see you tomorrow," I called out to Lyle when the last customer had left the building. "Be sure to lock the back door, okay?"

"Yeah, got it." He nodded and waved from behind the counter.

I grabbed my purse and headed down the street with an errand list clutched in my fist. Since Dad rarely left the house, the bulk of the shopping fell to me. Twice a week, between running the coffee shop and taking online business courses, I found time to hit the groceries and drug stores. I scanned the list of items scrawled in my father's small, tight handwriting. Shaving cream, razor blades, dental floss, and red licorice. I shook my head and smiled. The toiletries were for him, but the red licorice was for me. Even in his depression, he still thought about me.

As I came out of the drug store, a brown tweed sport jacket caught my eye. My heart leaped into my throat. I knew that coat and the dark-haired man who wore it. It was Harold, striding along the sidewalk, alone and confident. He paused in front of the cigar shop before going inside. I ducked into an alley, placing a hand on my chest, and struggled to maintain my cool. Part of me wanted to confront him. The other part, knew better. I'd already tried that and had spent a night in jail for my efforts.

Once my pulse returned to normal, I donned the cheap, blond wig I'd purchased online and an oversized pair of black sunglasses. Things I kept in my bag to use whenever the opportunity presented itself. I drew in a deep breath. This was either crazy or brave. I had no idea which. All I knew was that I couldn't afford to get caught again.

When Harold exited the store, I tailed him, taking care to stay at a reasonable distance. At the end of the block, he met a tall, thin woman with shiny hair and a long nose. I hid behind a Dumpster and peered around the side. They hugged then shared a lingering kiss. This was the girl who'd stolen my place. I wrinkled my nose in distaste then sucked in a horrified breath. Zipper, my sweet terrier mutt, danced at the woman's feet on the end of a rhinestone studded leash. I blinked back tears of happiness and dismay. At least the little guy was okay. Did he miss me? It took all my self-control to keep from snatching the dog and running away with him.

"What're you doing?" A familiar male voice rumbled in my left ear.

My heartbeat thundered. I placed a hand on my chest, breathing through the fright. "Nothing."

Carter's golden eyes roved over the wig, staring through the dark lenses of the sunglasses, amusement obvious in the lines around his mouth. I tried to push past him, mortified beyond belief, but he blocked my path with an outstretched arm. "Oh, you're definitely up to something. Care to let me in on the fun?"

"Go away." I tried to shoo him into the street, but he didn't budge. "You're going to ruin everything." In the meantime, Harold and his floozy began to walk in the opposite direction. I shoved Carter aside, eager to keep my dog in sight. How could I stay anonymous with a long-haired tattooed sex god at my side? Every female pair of eyes—and a few male—turned to watch him.

"Ruin what?" he asked, falling into step beside me.

The couple stopped at the crosswalk to the park. I ducked into the gap between two buildings, tugging Carter into the narrow space with me. His laughter echoed against the brick walls.

"Is this some kind of game? Because I like it."

"Hush." I tried hard to ignore the press of his hard chest against my shoulders, the firm lines of his muscles, the bite of his belt buckle into my back.

He peered over my shoulder, following my gaze. When Harold stepped into the street, I bolted after them, careful to keep my distance. Carter kept pace beside me, his long legs matching the stride of my shorter ones.

"You're following them, aren't you?" His bright eyes scoured my face. "Why, you little stalker you." The mirth in his voice ruffled my self-restraint.

I punched him in the shoulder. "Shut up. Seriously."

Harold and his fiancée passed through the park gate. The girl unhooked the leash from Zipper's collar. He gave a joyful yip and ran in circles around their feet. Tears burned my eyes. He'd been my dog for the past ten years. Mine. I'd nursed him from a bottle as a puppy, prayed for him when he'd been hit by a car, and let him sleep beneath the covers of my bed every night until Harold had stolen him.

Seeing my distress, Carter sobered. "Who are they?"

"The guy is my ex. The girl is his fiancée." I stared across the park, watching Zipper harass the pigeons while Harold held his fiancée's hand. It was like watching an alternate universe. That should have been my life. I should have been sitting in the park with my fiancé and my dog instead of slaving away behind a counter, pouring coffee, and tending to my middle-aged father. I lifted my chin, determined to maintain my dignity. "We had a—a—difficult breakup."

"Oh, I get it." He shoved his hands into his pockets. A whisper of wind lifted the leaves overhead, swirling the sweet scent of honeysuckle around us.

"No. You don't." How could I explain this complicated mess to someone like him? He'd never understand. Hell, I didn't understand. Harold took his fiancée's hand, whistled to Zipper, and they disappeared through the gate on the opposite side of the park. I dropped my head into my hands.

"Sure I do. He dumped you. Now, you're obsessed and you want him back." His eyes narrowed. "You're not planning to knock him off, are you?"

"No." I sank onto the nearest bench and pulled off the wig. Carter sat beside me, stretching his long legs out in front of him, resting his arms across the bench behind us. His bicep brushed the nape of my neck, sending a thrill down my spine.

"I hate to point out the obvious, but stalking the guy isn't going to work." I shifted away from his arm, but the heat of his body shimmered down my side. Even when we weren't touching, I could still feel him. "You know that, right?"

I didn't answer, taking a few minutes to formulate a response. When Mom had died, there hadn't been time to think about anything but holding my family together. Dad had fallen into a funk and had never recovered. Bronte had a new and successful career, and now a boyfriend. I'd taken over the coffee shop and had put every ounce of effort into keeping it alive, because there wasn't anyone else to do it. Harold hadn't understood the importance of my family. He'd resented the time I spent at work, my father's illness, Bronte's special needs. How could I love a man who'd left me when I needed him the most?

"It's complicated." To avoid Carter's scrutiny, I concentrated on the hem of my shirt, toying with the fabric. He probably thought I was crazy, and maybe I was.

The hard length of his thigh bumped against my leg, alighting my nerve endings. "I've got plenty of time."

CHAPTER 9
CARTER

The air chilled and ruffled through the branches of the trees. Jo stared straight ahead. God, she was lovely in the afternoon light. An errant ray of sun illuminated the auburn highlights in her dark hair. A stray lock dangled over one eye, fluttering on the light breeze. I brushed the silky strand behind her ear, feeling a shiver course through my fingers at the touch of her skin against mine.

"I don't want to talk about it." The line of her jaw set stubbornly, but unshed tears glimmered in her eyes. "He dumped me. He doesn't love me. End of story."

What kind of fucker wouldn't love her? Anger flared in my chest. "Then he's a fool," I said. I hated the bastard for making her cry. I hated the way her lower lip quivered. I hated the way her tears made me feel helpless. "You're a force to be reckoned with, Jo Hollander, and if he can't see you the way I see you—amazing, strong, determined—then he's an idiot."

"Obviously." Her eyes met mine, still shiny with hurt. She lifted her chin higher.

"You want me to go over there and punch him?" I said, only half joking.

"No." She recoiled, then a tiny smile tilted the corners of her lips. "Well, yes, that would be awesome, but no. He's not worth it."

"If you change your mind, let me know." I flexed my fingers, thinking how good it would feel to break that skinny guy's straight nose. I'd taken an instant dislike to his stuffy blazer, the scarf around his neck, and his shiny loafers.

"Let's go." She stood, all traces of tears gone from her cheeks and a steely strength straightening her shoulders. "This was a waste of time. Can you take me home?"

We made the trip in silence. When I pulled the vehicle into her driveway, I shut off the engine and faced her. She smiled, but I saw through the façade. I hated seeing her so upset but admired the way she fought to be brave. Our eyes met. No matter how hard I tried, I couldn't look away. I wanted to take her in my arms, suck her full bottom lip into my mouth, and never let it go.

"Well, thanks for the ride." Her hand reached for the door handle, spurring me into action.

"Hold up." I hopped out of the car, jogged to the other side, and opened the door. On the way, I passed her car, still sitting in the same place. "What's up with your ride?"

"The transmission is out." A heavy sigh lifted her boobs. I tried not to stare. "It's low on my list of priorities right now."

"I could take a look at it if you want." The offer popped out before I could stop it. "I'm not a mechanic, but I know my way around a car."

"Thanks, but no. You've done more than enough."

"I know I don't have to. I want to." And there it was, plain and simple. I *wanted* to help her. "Besides, I enjoy it." I extended a hand to help her down from the seat then closed the door behind her.

"Well, I suppose you can't mess it up any worse than it already is."

"Your confidence is underwhelming."

We both laughed. I placed a hand below her shoulders, guiding her around the front of the car, toward the house. Her dad met us at the front door. Like before, he was wearing a white T-shirt and boxer shorts.

"What's going on? Is everything okay?" he asked, eyeing me suspiciously, his gaze bouncing from Jo's red-rimmed eyes to my face.

"Everything's fine, Dad. Get in the house before the neighbors see you." She flapped a hand, her cheeks flushing with embarrassment.

"I thought you two weren't dating." His eyes met mine, eyes exactly like Jo's and full of fatherly protectiveness.

"We're not," Jo and I said in unison.

"He gave me a lift home from the coffee shop," she continued. "He's going to check out my car."

"If you don't mind," I added, not wanting to step on his authority as man of the house.

"I don't mind," he said. "I've got a hydraulic lift. You can put it up and take a look."

Two car doors slammed in the driveway. The three of us snapped our heads in the direction of the sounds. Bronte's red head appeared on the other side of the screen door, followed by Rhett's brown one.

"Hey, Dad." Bronte planted a kiss on her father's cheek then narrowed her eyes at my hand on Jo's back. I pulled it away and used it to ruffle my hair. I hadn't even realized I was still touching her; it had felt so right there. Jo stepped aside, widening the gap between us. Bronte's gaze bounced between me and her sister. "What are you guys doing?"

"Yeah, what are you doing here?" Rhett lifted an eyebrow at me. "Hey, Mr. H. Good to see you."

"I gave her a ride home," I said, feeling like I'd been caught with my hand in the cookie jar.

"Carter's going to take a look at my car," Jo said, her flush deepening from rose to scarlet.

"I'll get the key to the garage," Mr. H said. "You boys wanna push the car down the driveway?"

"Sure," I said with a slow shake of my head for Rhett. Whatever he was thinking, he needed to keep it to himself.

"You guys want a beer?" Jo asked, moving toward the kitchen. Mr. H followed her, his step lighter than before. Jo extended an arm, blocking his path. "For God's sake, Dad, put on some pants, would you?"

A chuckle bounced up my throat. I coughed and cleared my throat to stifle it. Rhett smirked, catching my gaze.

Mr. H disappeared into the laundry room and came out wearing a pair of well-worn blue jeans and a gray T-shirt. Fully dressed, he looked less broken and younger. He dangled a set of keys from his hand. "Come on, boys. Let's take a look at that car."

———

Mr. H had a three-bay fully equipped garage behind the house. When he lifted the middle overhead door, Rhett let out a low whistle. A 1967 Oldsmobile 442 sat in the left bay. I made a straight line to it and trailed a hand over the front fender.

"You like that?" Mr. H asked.

"Hell yes. Who wouldn't?" I bent to peer through the dusty window.

"All original from bumper to bumper." The pride in the man's voice was unmistakable. "Only forty thousand miles on it. Needs some work though."

"It's a shame to see it just sitting here," Rhett said. We stared at the car in admiration. "Why don't you fix it up?"

"I bought it for my wife. She had a car just like this when we met." His shoulders dipped and the light left his eyes. "After she was gone, I didn't see much use in it anymore. Too many memories."

"Rhett and I worked at a garage, changing oil and doing tune-ups when were in high school." I jumped to another topic of conversation, hoping to ease his distress. "You've got a nice setup in here."

"Thanks. When I was younger, I spent a lot of time out here, when cars were simple. I'm not much with new ones." He turned away from the Oldsmobile and back to Jo's car. "I'll try to help if I can though."

"Sounds like a plan." Rhett nodded toward the dilapidated Chevy. "Let's get her on the lift and see what's going on."

Mr. H took the wheel while Rhett and I pushed the car from the rear. I could tell Rhett had something to say by the way his eyes sparkled. When Mr. H stepped away to activate the lift, Rhett searched my face.

"Don't look at me like that," I said, frowning.

"What are you up to?"

"Nothing. Can't a guy help a girl out?" I tried to walk past him, but he stepped into my path.

"You don't do anything without an agenda. It's not the way you're built." When I tried to go around him again, he put a hand on my arm. "Don't mess with my family, Carter."

"I'm not messing with them." His accusation stung. Did he really think I'd stoop so low?

"Then what are you doing here? With Jo? Look me in the eyes and tell me you're not up to something."

I clenched my jaw before staring him straight in the eyes. "I'm not up to anything. I like Jo. She needs some help. I can help her. Give me a fucking break." We glared at each other. "I mean it."

"Okay." His hand dropped to his side, tone wary.

Jo entered the garage, carrying a tray of canned beers and snacks. The swing of her round bottom redirected my attention. Rhett saw the trajectory of my gaze and scowled. I looked back at Jo. This time all I saw were her long-lashed eyes. They stared at me and into me, clear and knowing and kind and filled with heat. I forgot to worry about Rhett or the car or Mr. H. I took the tray from Jo, rewarded by her smile, and grinned back.

"Jesus, Carter," Rhett muttered under his breath, still at my side. "You promised."

"Well, I'm unpromising," I replied, my gaze continuing to follow Jo as she stood beside her dad. I rarely, if ever, went back on a promise, but this one I couldn't keep. I wanted Jo Hollander in my bed, and no one, not even my best friend, could stop me from trying to get her there.

CHAPTER 10

JO

The past few years of my life had been filled with tragedy and sadness, but the sight of my dad laughing with Carter and Rhett, grease smudged on his cheek, and a spring in his step, brought a lightness to my heart I hadn't thought possible. My sister and I retreated to the sidelines, watching the miracle with awe. Testosterone filled the garage. Deep male laughter echoed between the walls. I drew in a steadying breath, reveling in the atmosphere.

"I can't believe it," Bronte said, shaking her head.

"It's amazing." The tunes of an upbeat pop song came on the radio. Dad tapped the toe of his shoe on the concrete floor.

"I haven't seen him smile like that since—" My sister's voice died away.

"I know." I stroked a hand down her soft hair. In this light, she looked so much like Mom, same upturned nose, same freckled skin. Everyone said that I resembled Mother the most while Bronte favored our father, but I could see a mixture of both parents in her features. I swallowed down a lump of nostalgia and happiness. "What about you? Are you happy? With Rhett, I mean?"

"Yes." The way her eyes lit up at the mention of his name

answered my questions. "He's good to me, Jo. Yesterday, I freaked out a little when a lady bumped our cart at the grocery store. He was so understanding. He took my hand and made me laugh. And he's always doing nice things for me, like bringing me chocolate, and he always, always puts the toilet seat down."

"I'm happy for you," I said. Little things meant so much to Bronte.

"And we have sex all the time. Constantly." Her smile brightened the shadowy corners of the garage. "He can't keep his hands off me."

As if sensing her words, Rhett glanced at Bronte from beneath the hood of the car and smiled. My chest swelled at the depth of affection in his gaze.

Although I was happy for her, I was a bit envious too. No man had ever been able to keep his hands off me, not even Harold. I wanted that kind of love for myself. The dream of my own home and family had withered and died with Mom. My future consisted of endless days and nights at the coffee shop and caring for Dad.

"What about you?" Bronte squeezed my hand. "I know you're not happy. You work too much, and you never go out anymore. Dad and I appreciate all that you've done for us, but it's time you take back your life."

"When?" The single word contained a world of frustration. "There's too much to do."

"I don't have the answers, but you need to make the time, Jo."

"I'm fine." I avoided her worried gaze, crossing my arms over my chest. Rhett continued to smile at Bronte. Carter glanced up from the engine to determine the source of his distraction. Our gazes collided with the impact of two speeding freight cars. An electrical charge ignited beneath my ribs, detonating tiny explosions of desire and lust. The smile slipped from Carter's face. He felt it—the friction and heat that came whenever our eyes met.

"Jo?" Bronte asked.

"What?" I tore my gaze from Carter and back to her. She arched an eyebrow. I frowned, trying to ignore the heat of embarrassment traveling up my neck. "Don't look at me like that."

"Are you guys fucking?" Her voice lifted in an excited squeal.

"No. Of course not."

"But you want to, right?" She clapped her hands together. "Yes! I told Rhett you guys were perfect for each other."

"Don't be silly." I rolled my eyes and pretended to study the wall.

"Come on. It's true. He likes casual sex. You hate relationships. It's a match made in heaven."

"Now you're being ridiculous." I took a sip of beer then pressed the cold can to my heated cheek. Carter passed in front of me. The scent of leather and beer mingled with male sweat and his cologne, acting like an aphrodisiac, making my muscles clench deep in my center. I followed him with my gaze, taking in the long lines of his legs, the tight stretch of his jeans over his hard ass.

"Am I?" Bronte shook her head. "You might be able to fool everyone else, but you can't fool me. You guys look at each other like the world is on fire."

"Right." I snorted, but her words gave me pause. At Rhett's request, Carter pulled a wrench from his back pocket and tossed it across the room. Rhett caught it with one hand then all three men reconvened beneath the hood. "Rhett made Carter promise not to sleep with me."

She scoffed and lowered her voice. "I'll take care of Rhett. I think you should go for it. Just don't fall in love, okay?"

We ordered pizza and ate in the garage, gathered around a fold-up table, the way we had when Mom had been alive. Back then, Dad had spent his free time in the garage, working on her car. There had been laughter and arguments and stolen kisses between them. After she'd passed, Dad had locked up the garage and had never gone back. It was good to see the place alive again, to see his smiles and hear his gruff voice.

Every time I looked in Carter's direction, he was staring back, sometimes smiling, sometimes not. The weight of his gaze made butterflies twirl in my stomach. What if Bronte was right? What if he was my perfect match? I shook my head at the crazy idea. Even though we'd become friends, he was still a pig, and I still hated men. Then again, what was the harm in a little flirtation, some guilt-free fooling around? Carter didn't want commitment or love or promises. He liked sex, and from what I'd seen of his body, he had to be pretty good at it.

When Rhett and Bronte left, my sister hugged me tightly and gave me a knowing smile. I squeezed her back, understanding passing between us. Once they were gone, Dad excused himself to the house.

"I'm going to bed," he said. "You kids have worn me out."

"Okay. Goodnight." I brushed away a smudge of grease from his chin with my thumb.

"Goodnight," Carter said. The two men shook hands.

"Thanks for the help," Dad said and clapped him on the shoulder. "You'll be back, right?"

"Yes. Rhett's going to order the parts, and we'll put them in." Carter spoke to Dad, but his gaze locked with mine.

I hopped onto the hood of the Oldsmobile and pressed my thighs together against the infinite ache of need.

"Excellent. Well, I'm heading to the house." Dad passed a meaningful glance between me and Carter. "I'm going straight to sleep, and I'll turn on the TV in my room. You're welcome to stay over, Carter. You kids make as much noise as you like."

"Dad." I rolled my eyes. Embarrassment scalded my cheeks.

With a wink to me, he closed the door behind him.

Carter laughed. "I love your old man. I hope I'm half as cool when I'm his age."

"I could die." I fanned my face with a pizza napkin. "He's usually not like that. I mean, he doesn't pimp me out to strangers."

"But I'm not a stranger anymore, am I?" He took the napkin from my hand and tossed it into the trash can.

My mouth went dry. "No," I croaked.

He placed one large hand on each of my knees, spread them wide, and stepped between them. With deliberate slowness, he brushed my hair over my shoulders and bared my neck. How many nights had I dreamed of him touching me in just this way? Our eyes met as he lowered his lips to my throat. His breath burned my skin. I moaned, wanting more.

"Do you have any idea how hard it's been to keep my hands off you today?" he asked.

"Not really." I clutched the car cover. The cool smoothness of the canvas contrasted with the roughness of his jeans between my thighs. "You've been hiding it pretty well."

"Such a smart ass." Soft lips pressed into mine. His tongue dipped inside my mouth, tasting of beer and pizza and spices. He drifted his hands over my shoulders and down my chest to cup both my breasts. The heat of his palms burned through the thin cotton of my shirt. I wanted to spontaneously combust.

"You've got the most beautiful tits I've ever seen." He squeezed gently. My pussy responded by clenching. "I got off in the shower this morning thinking about them."

"I wish I could have seen that." I closed my eyes, picturing him naked beneath a stream of steaming water, his dick in his hand, grunting my name. The thought turned my knees to jelly.

"I think about fucking them." He pushed my breasts together and ran his tongue along the line of my cleavage. I nearly fainted from the combination of wetness and heat. He placed a kiss on the hollow above my clavicle. I tilted my head, allowing his lips to travel higher, up to my jaw.

"Is that the only thing you want to fuck?" My voice returned, along with my courage. I pulled the elastic from his hair. The thick locks spilled over his shoulders. The movement released the citrusy scent of his shampoo.

We stared at each other. His nostrils flared. I wrapped his hair around my left fist and tugged hard. His growl snapped my self-control in half. If I was going to do this, it had to be now, before I lost my nerve.

With both hands, I lifted the hem of my shirt over my head. Carter's gaze ran over my body. My skin burned everywhere his eyes landed. Together we pulled his shirt off. The skin of his chest was smooth, his nipples small and flat. I drank in every inch of his bare flesh down to the star tattoo below his left hipbone. "You're perfect," I said.

"Far from it," he replied. "But you—you're better than perfect, better than my dreams." With a fingertip, he explored the swells of my breasts, along the lacy edge of my bra. "Take this off. Let me see you."

I reached behind my back and unclasped the bra with a flick of my fingers. He lowered the straps down over my shoulders. My breasts fell free. Cool air breezed over my naked flesh. With one hand, he cupped the left breast, lifting it, testing the weight in his hand. The pad of his thumb brushed over the nipple. I hissed at the sting of arousal.

"I need to taste this." He bent and drew one pale pink nipple into his mouth. I smoothed my hands down his back and arched into him. "Mmmm...sweet," he murmured, his breath scalding the sensitive skin. He began to suck. Each flick of his tongue over the tip sent a pang of need deep into my center. I cupped the nape of his neck to keep him near, and gave myself over to the pleasure of being touched.

"What about Rhett? Your promise?"

"Screw that. Deal's off. I told him today."

Our harsh breathing filled the silence. Carter yanked down my pants. I fumbled with his zipper, freeing the length of his long, hard cock. It sprang forward into my hand. "Condom?" I asked.

"Wallet. Back pocket."

Of course he'd be prepared. I tried not to dwell on the fact that he'd been with a lot of women before me and there would be many more to follow. My focus remained on the present, on the feel of his calloused hands on my body, the strength of his thighs as he spread mine wider, the scrape of his beard over my bare skin. This was about sex, not feelings. I needed this release. I felt wild, wanton. We pulled apart long enough for him to slide the condom over his shaft, and then we snapped back together.

"I'm going to let you fuck me," I said, meaning every word of it. "And you'd better make it good, because it's never going to happen again."

CHAPTER 11
CARTER

"Carter." She said my name, desperate and needy, drawing my attention back to her face. Then she pulled my hair, hard enough to make me grunt. God, I loved a woman who took charge during sex. "Do it now."

With both hands on her ass, I lifted her onto my cock. She was so wet; I slid inside easily. We moaned in tandem. The tight, hot walls of her pussy clenched around me. I wanted to hammer into her, but I forced myself to pause for a second and gather my sensibilities.

She tugged on my hair again, harder. I hissed at the pleasure-pain. "What are you waiting for?" she asked.

"Easy, baby." I murmured the words against the tiny shell of her ear. Her breasts rose and fell, her breathing ragged. She was wound up tight for me. I pushed further inside, giving her all of me, and held there. Her nails dug into my shoulders. "God, you feel unbelievable."

"So do you." The tip of her tongue slid across her trembling lower lip.

"One of these days, I'm going to fuck that smart mouth." I ran the tip of my nose along the column of her neck, drinking in her delicious scent, nibbling the galloping pulse at the base of her jaw.

"Yes." Her pupils dilated until her eyes looked black. "What else will you do?"

"I'll taste you here." I placed my thumb on her clit and rubbed a small circle. Her head tipped back, eyelids lowering. "Would you like that?"

"Yes. Oh, God yes." She undulated her hips, moving when I wouldn't, taking control. I followed her lead, rotating my pelvis to match her pace. We fit together perfectly. I pulled out all the way then slid home again with a sharp thrust. She yelped in surprise then smiled. "Yes. That. Again."

We fucked like animals on the hood of the car. Our skin slapped together. Our grunts and the smell of sex filled the air. I hammered into her over and over and over until I forgot to worry about anything but her. She clung to me, raked my skin with her nails, called out my name like I was a god. The muscles in my legs strained from the effort. It was perfect and raw and unnerving.

"I'm going to come," I said when the white-hot flash of pre-release licked up my legs. My words sent her pussy into spasms. She clutched and fluttered around my cock. I picked her up, pushing into her until I thought she might split in two. She wrapped her legs around my waist, her cries breaking the night silence. "Give me your mouth, Jo. Now." Our mouths came together for the first time tonight. I silenced her whimpers with my lips and tongue. My balls tightened, and I lost all sense of time and space.

When I finally started to come down from the euphoria, I realized she was completely naked, my pants were around my ankles, and we were standing in the center of the garage. My body trembled like I'd run a marathon, muscles spent and aching. I set her gently onto the hood of the car, afraid I might drop her. Her legs slipped from my waist. We stared at each other.

She broke the silence first, tearing her eyes from me and scanning the floor for her clothes. "Well, I guess I'd better get inside. I've got to get to work early."

And that was it. We both got dressed. I walked her to the house.

She went inside, and I went home. It should have ended there. One night. One fuck. No expectations. It should have, but it didn't, not for me.

———

The next morning, I wanted to call her. God knew why. It went against all my rules. No phone calls. No sleeping over. No dates. The list went on and on. During my adult life, I'd stuck to those guidelines like they were written in stone. A dozen times throughout the day, I brought up her number on my phone, and a dozen times I cancelled it. God, what was wrong with me?

I never intended to let things go so far with Jo, but my attraction had morphed into an obsession. That night, I fell asleep with my dick in my hand, dreamed of her pretty tits, and awoke with a raging erection. I thought one encounter would be enough, that the fantasies would melt away like they had with every other girl I'd been with. I didn't expect her skin to smell and taste like cotton candy. I didn't think the reality of her would far exceed the fantasy. Instead of cleansing her from my system, I'd added fuel to the fire, making it burn brighter and more intensely.

I trudged through work, processing bonds, following up on clients, and sifting through leads on bail jumpers. Later that night, I headed to my favorite watering hole. Maybe I could find a pretty face to erase the picture of Jo in my head and the feel of her on my cock. No one compared, however. Not the pretty bartender or the group of college girls sending flirtatious smiles in my direction or the businesswoman in the corner who sent me a drink. After a couple of beers, I headed home, more restless than when I began, and stared at the TV.

My phone taunted me. What was she doing? It was close to ten o'clock. She was probably in bed, since she went to work so early in the morning. My thumb hovered over her name in my contact list.

Before I could second guess my actions, I typed out a quick text. Texting wasn't calling, so technically, I wasn't breaking my rules.

Me: Are you awake?

I stared at the phone, wishing I could take it back. What if she thought I was an idiot? Hell, I *was* an idiot, acting like a teenager, obsessing over our one-off. Eager for a distraction, I headed to my bedroom and placed the phone on the nightstand. Following a cold shower, I climbed into bed. The phone buzzed just as I snapped off the light.

Jo: What's up?

My heart raced and my mouth went dry. Aside from the occasional drunk text the only women I texted were my mom, Darcy, and Reagan. Now that I had Jo's attention, I had no idea what to say. Moisture gathered on my palms. I waited a few seconds, not wanting to appear overeager.

Me: Are you in bed?

Jo: Yes, are you?

Me: Yes.

Jo: Alone?

I read and reread her message, trying to deduce her mood, her motives. The minds of women had always eluded me, and I'd never stuck around long enough to learn anything about them other than how to get them off. Had I opened a Pandora's box by screwing her in the garage, by contacting her again? The Jo I knew didn't give a flying fuck about having a relationship. So what if she had an unhealthy obsession with her ex? It had nothing to do with me. If anything, it let me off the hook. This thought eased my misgivings. By her own admission, she was out for a good time and nothing else. Maybe I should call her bluff, as a test.

Me: I've got a hot brunette in my bed and she's begging me to fuck her.

Her reply came immediately, and it wasn't at all what I expected.

Jo: What are you going to do to her? Tell me.

Something tightened low in my gut. I sat up, interest flaring. I typed out an answer, erased it, and started again.

Me: *I've got her stripped naked and I'm sucking on her tits.*

Jo: *What a coincidence. I'm naked too.*

I dropped the phone. Damn. A flash of her stretched out on the bed lit up my imagination, perky tits in the air, nipples straining skyward, and the sexy V of her pussy staring back at me. Blood rushed into my cock, leaving my thoughts clouded, making the room spin.

Me: *Calling.*

She answered before the first ring ended. Fuck my stupid rules.

"Are you really naked?" I asked.

"Yes. And I'm touching myself." On the phone, her voice sounded lower, huskier, seductive. "I'm so horny, Carter."

My reservations withered and died. "Where?" My voice broke. "Where are you touching yourself?"

"I'm tugging on my nipples." A tiny moan followed the hitch of her breath.

"Are you wet?" My cock stiffened to the point of pain. I shifted to ease some of the pressure, leaning forward, wishing I could see her. The joints of my fingers ached from gripping the phone.

"No fair. It's your turn. I want to know if you're hard."

"God, yes." The outline of my erection strained against the cotton of my boxer briefs. I dragged my palm along the length of it.

"Are you touching it?" Her voice was soft, intimate. "Is *she* touching it?"

So, that was her game. Little Jo Hollander wanted it dirty. This was her lucky day, because I did too. "Yeah. She's sucking me, running her tongue up and down my shaft." I shoved my hand inside my underwear and stroked my cock. The vein on the underside pulsed.

"Do you like it?" The lazy purr of her words made my balls tighten. "Does her mouth feel good?"

"I'd enjoy it more if it was your mouth."

"Me too."

"I'm coming over."

"No." The sharp refusal brought my hand to a standstill. "You can't. It's late. Dad's asleep, and you'd wake him up."

"I want to see you," I said. "I'm so fucking hard I can't stand it. Let me come over, Jo." I'd never begged a woman for sex before, but I had no problems doing it now. If she asked, I'd crawl on my knees for it.

"Don't worry. I'll take care of you." The promise in her words eased my anxiety while stoking my orgasm. "Listen to my voice. Are you listening, Carter?"

"Yes." Every word, every breath, drew me deeper into a new kind of hell, one where only Jo and I existed.

"I've got my fingers in my pussy. I'm rubbing my thumb over my clit, and it feels so good. I wish it was your tongue."

"You're killing me," I growled and thrust into my fist, the need to come unbearable. "I bet you taste great."

"Do you think about me, Carter? Do you think about putting your mouth on me? Tasting me?" Her harsh breathing carried across the air waves. She was hovering at the brink and so was I.

"Yes. I want to put my tongue inside you, lick you until you squirm." My balls tightened, and a warning tingle jolted down my legs. "God, I'm so close."

"Me, too. I'm almost there."

"Put another finger inside you." I couldn't think, couldn't breathe. Time stood still. The world consisted of my cock and her coaxing, teasing, angelic voice. Sweat beaded across my forehead. I squeezed my eyes shut. "Pretend it's my dick. I'm fucking you hard."

"Oh, God. Yes. Yes." Her breathing stuttered, and the sweetest moan I'd ever heard brought me to climax. "I'm coming, Carter."

"Fuck. Jo." I groaned, low and deep, milking my shaft. The powerful orgasm shook my body. My thighs twitched and my legs jerked. Until now, sex had been a routine act to escape boredom or release anger. Never had it been this cathartic. I collapsed against the pillow, amazed and disoriented. "Jesus."

"That was unbelievable," she said in a breathy whisper. Her voice turned lazy and sated, like a kitten who'd drank too much cream. "I'm exhausted."

"Yeah, me too." The tension in my muscles faded away, replaced by warmth. My eyelids sagged. "Damn, I didn't know you had that in you. I've seriously underestimated you, Hollander."

"I need to go." In the space of a few heartbeats, her voice turned distant. Wasn't that what I wanted? No commitment. Just sex. I repeated the words over and over in my head. If this was the perfect scenario, then why did I feel so disappointed to end the call?

"Sleep tight, kitten," I said.

"Good night, Carter."

———

I t took all my self-control to stay away from the coffee shop the next day and the day after that. I went to my mom's house instead. She lived in an extravagant home on the upper west side. I hated going there, but I did it anyway, because she was my mom, and I loved her. The guard at the entrance to Forest Hills waved me through the tall, wrought iron gates. I followed the curving drive past manicured lawns, enormous houses, and a snooty golf course.

Mom met me at the front door, all smiles and tears. "Where have you been? It's been ages. I was just telling your father that you never call or come over anymore. Give your mother a hug."

Funny how a five-foot-nothing woman could make me feel small. "Sorry. Business. You know." I wrapped my arms around her petite frame and lifted her off the floor. She laughed and pressed a kiss to my cheek.

"Put me down, you big lug." She wriggled until I set her gently on the marble tiles.

"You look nice," I said, holding her at arm's length and giving her the once over. At forty-eight she was still a handsome woman, trim and curvaceous. When I was a kid, my friends had loved to visit my house to see Honey Wilkes, my "hot mom," the MILF who'd starred in a rock music video. "Is this a new dress?"

"Do you like it?" She smoothed her hands over the skirt.

"Very nice. Are you going somewhere? Did I come at a bad time?" The moment I spoke, I wished I could retract the questions. She avoided my gaze, but her secretive smile was the only answer I needed. The hairs on the back of my neck bristled. "Is *he* coming over?"

"Yes. He should be here any minute." Excitement lilted her words. She brushed her hands through her hair, turning to preen in the mirror beside us.

Sometimes I hated my mom. The way she hung on my father's every word. The way she lived to please him. Mostly, I hated my father, because he didn't give a shit about her. He didn't care that she spent his money on clothes and plastic surgery in an effort to keep his attention. He didn't care that she waited by the phone for hours, hoping he'd call or toss a morsel of affection in her direction. All he wanted was a warm and willing woman in his bed whenever or wherever he dictated.

"Mom, why are you still with this guy? He's a dick. You don't need him. Give him the boot."

She laughed and rolled her eyes. "Oh, Carter, don't be silly. I'll never leave your father."

"Is it the money?" I caught her hand in mine, forcing her to look at me. "Because you don't need it. I'll take care of you. I have more than enough for the both of us."

"Carter, stop it." Her tone turned angry. She pulled her hand from mine, her expression hardening. "It's not about the money. I don't expect you to understand. You've never been in love."

"The way he treats you—that's not love," I growled.

"Not another word." After a deep breath, her features relaxed, a well-rehearsed softness replacing the irritation. "This is going to be wonderful. I can't wait to have both my men in the house at the same time." She turned enormous, hopeful blue eyes up to me. "Say you'll stay."

"Okay." I could never disappoint her. That was *his* job. "Just for a little while."

I didn't have time to leave anyway, because the door latch clicked two seconds later and my father walked into the foyer, looking imposing in an immaculate black suit, white shirt, and red tie. If I had my way, I'd deny any relationship to him, but it was impossible when I was a carbon copy of him. He turned gold-brown eyes to me and lifted an eyebrow in his signature smartass smirk. I was taller by an inch or two, so I stared down my nose at him, refusing to be intimidated.

"Well, look what the cat dragged in." The predatory gaze raked over my long hair, beard, and cargo pants, brimming with disapproval. "Hello, Honey." He leaned in so Mom could kiss his cheek. She hovered around him like a butterfly, taking his suit jacket, loosening his tie, peppering his cheek with kisses. He shooed her away with a wave of his fingers. Hurt flickered in her eyes. "Get me a scotch, would you, babe?"

Hatred bubbled through my veins. His casual dismissal scraped over my nerves like sandpaper. I was used to being derided and ignored. Watching him degrade my mother was another thing entirely. He pushed past me and moved into the living room, his polished Italian shoes thudding softly on the tile, their shiny black leather reflecting the gilt surfaces and brilliant chandeliers overhead.

"Sit, Mom. I'll get it." I took her by the elbow and guided her toward the sofa.

"Oh, you're so good to me," she said, smiling again. "Thank you. I'll have a vodka tonic please."

I went to the bar, happy for the distraction. By the time I was ten years old, I'd become an accomplished bartender, serving at my mother's cocktail parties, amusing her bohemian guests. She sat beside my father, one hand on his forearm, the other stroking his hair. I watched their reflections in the bar mirror. My father pulled her in tight for a deep kiss. My stomach twisted.

"I need you to pack a bag, Honey. I booked you a room at my hotel in Monte Carlo. I've got some business there, and I want you with me," he said.

"Oh, I can't wait. I've never been to Monte Carlo." Mom beamed up at him. I understood what this meant. She'd be squirreled away in a hotel room, waiting for his beck and call, while he ignored her.

He smoothed his tie and smiled down at her before shifting his gaze back to me. "So to what do I owe this honor, Carter?"

"I'm here to see Mom, not you."

"Carter." Mom frowned, adding to my unease. It was one thing to irritate my father, another thing to upset her. "Be nice."

I handed their drinks to them and poured two fingers of tequila for myself. I didn't usually drink this early in the day, but encounters with my father called for an exception.

"It's okay, Honey. I wouldn't expect any less from him." Sunlight shafted through the velvet drapes and caught the silver threads in his brown hair when he cocked his head. "Still chasing the bad guys? I heard about Benson. Great job. You took a predator off the street."

"Thanks." I choked back a lifetime of resentment for Mom's sake. "I'm surprised you noticed."

"I like to know what my family is up to." His fingers stroked along my mother's thigh. "You're doing quite well with your business, I hear."

"It's fine." I bristled, instantly on the defensive.

"And you invested in an apartment complex. I see you're putting my money to good use."

"My money," I replied, leveling my gaze on his.

My mother, for all her flaws, had insisted on a paternity test when she'd become pregnant. After lengthy negotiations, my father had set aside a trust fund for me—a very big, very generous sum. The money meant nothing to him; he was one of the wealthiest men in the country. His marriage and political career, however, meant everything. I became the dirty little secret, the bastard son of a senator and his mistress.

"Right," he said. He turned to my mom and stroked a hand down her cheek. "I'm going upstairs. Say goodbye to Carter and be quick. I've only got an hour." With a little growl, he smacked her on the ass, making her squeal. My fingers curled into fists. Why couldn't she see through his actions? Why did she let him treat her like a whore? A dozen times before, I'd begged her to leave him, but she'd only laughed, giving me the brush off like today.

"Okay." Mom didn't even look at me. "Bye-bye, Carter. Call me, sweetie."

"I'll show myself out," I said to no one in particular, because they were already moving up the stairs.

I sat in my car for a few minutes before I left, too angry to be on the road. This was the reason I didn't do relationships. This was the reason I never spent the night with a woman, and this was the reason I never called the next day. Because no one would ever use me the way my father used my mother. No one. She loved him with some kind of misguided, lopsided obsession. Watching her love him killed me in a way I hadn't known possible, because he didn't love her back. He didn't love anyone but himself.

CHAPTER 12
JO

The days passed in a haze of broken espresso machines, late bakery deliveries, and past due utility bills. I struggled to make ends meet, keeping the problems of the coffee shop to myself, not wanting to burden my father. In the few spare moments I managed to scrape together, my thoughts turned to Carter, our glorious fuck in the garage, and our naughty phone sex. I replayed them over and over in my head, wearing them out until they were faded and thin like an old letter. Those moments had been hot, dirty, and perfect; everything I needed. So why did I want more? Why couldn't I be content to let things stand?

At night, I left my phone by the bed, waiting for Carter's late night text, the one that never came. I wasn't sure why. I didn't want a relationship with him. Loneliness fueled my fantasies. A couple of times, I opened a text message to him but deleted it before sending. Did I really want to start something I had no intention of finishing? By the next morning, I managed to convince myself that it was for the best.

After I closed shop on Friday, I met Bronte and Rhett at a local diner for a late lunch. They were crammed into a small booth by the front window. In the seat across from the couple, a familiar head and broad shoulders rose above the backrest of the bench. My heart skipped a beat. Shuttered brown eyes met mine; the flecks of gold dimmed. My initial excitement at seeing him fizzled and sputtered into confusion.

"Hey," I said lightly and slid into the seat beside him. I rubbed sweaty palms over my denim skirt. Turbulence rolled off him in waves, causing my stomach to churn.

"Hey, sis." Bronte smiled at me. Carter grunted and stared straight ahead. Rhett nodded, his mouth full of buttermilk biscuit.

We talked about the weather, sports scores, and the latest Hollywood scandal. Or, I should say, the three of us talked. Carter remained mute. His broody silence filled the space between us until I wanted to scream from the tension. At the end of the meal, he picked up the tab for everyone and headed toward the restroom at the back of the diner. I said goodbye to Rhett and Bronte before following him.

I leaned against the wall in the hallway and waited for him to come out. Had I done something wrong? Was he angry about the way we'd left things? In my opinion, the hookup had been perfect, but maybe he didn't feel the same way. My temper simmered at a low boil, threatening to overflow. It was his idea to be friends. If we were going to continue hanging out with Rhett and Bronte, I needed answers.

The bathroom door opened, and Carter came out. He froze, startled by my appearance, before brushing past me. I stopped him with a hand on his arm.

"What's the deal?" I asked. "You haven't spoken to me since I got here. Are you mad at me?"

"No." His lion eyes leveled on me, still blank, still shuttered.

"Then why are you being rude? If it's because of what happened the other night, you can stop worrying. I'm not one of those clingy types. It was good. Better than good. But it's not going to happen again."

"Okay." One corner of his mouth trembled, like he wanted to smile but couldn't quite make the leap.

"Alright then." My hands shook. I pressed them against my hips so he wouldn't see.

"I've got some shit going on," he said, cocking his head. "But none of it has anything to do with you." At the base of his neck, his pulse pounded, sure and steady. I wanted to press a kiss there. It took all of my self-control to stop myself. He moistened his lips, his gaze thirsty. "The phone sex—it was a real surprise." His voice dropped lower, scratching the itch deep inside me. "I liked it."

The walls of the narrow hallway pressed in on us. Only a few inches existed between my breasts and the hard muscles of his chest. To the left was the kitchen, to the right a coat rack, and at my back was a closet door. Carter filled the remaining space. My skin tingled from his proximity.

Oh, no. No. I swallowed against the dryness in my mouth. His gaze dipped to my lips and slowly crawled to my eyes. Lightning zipped into my core. *No, no, no.* I drew in a deep breath, trying to center myself, and got a lungful of leather and citrus. My inner walls clenched, hard enough to make my thighs tremble. I bit the inside of my cheek, hoping the pain would extinguish the sexual attraction coursing through my veins.

"No." I whispered the word aloud, as a warning to myself, while my body screamed *yes*.

"Yes," he replied, his voice cracked and broken. It was only one word, but I knew exactly what he meant. He felt it too, the strong pull of desire. It happened every time he came around; all the promises I made to myself flew out the window.

"Yes." I repeated, entranced by his closeness.

One of his hands slipped behind my waist and turned the door-knob. The door gave way on silent hinges. He walked me backward into the closet. The door closed. Once my eyes adjusted to the dim light, I could make out the shapes of brooms and dustpans and shelves lined with cleaners.

"Are you sure?" he asked. His big hands roamed down my arms, along my ribcage, up my back.

"Yes." Oh, Lord, I'd never been more certain in my life. My panties were soaked at the thought, my body brought to life by his touch.

Someone walked down the hall and paused outside the closet door. We stilled, our eyes meeting in understanding. This needed to be stealthy and silent. His chest flattened my breasts. The hard outline of his erection bit into my belly. One of his hands slipped beneath my skirt. The tip of his finger drew the cotton panel of my panties aside and slipped through my slick folds.

"Jesus, kitten," he murmured in my ear, so quietly I sensed his words more than I heard them. The intrusion of his roughened fingertip made me forget to be mute.

"Ah, Carter, yes."

"You have to be quiet," he whispered against my neck. The plush stiffness of his beard tickled my jaw.

"Then you'd better hurry up or all bets are off." I palmed the length of his cock, straining against his jeans.

"You're my kind of girl." His smile brushed my neck. "Condom. Back pocket."

I slid my hands down his spine to the wallet in his back pocket. By feel, I found the condom and ripped the foil packet. While he teased my clit, I drew the condom over the length of his cock. My body hummed with desire, taut as a guitar string. In the hallway, the bathroom door opened and closed. We held our collective breaths and exhaled in tandem when the footsteps faded away. The danger of getting caught heightened the excitement. I'd never done in anything so risky or quite this dirty, and I loved it.

He stared into my eyes. With a hand on each of my hips, he shoved inside me with a muffled grunt. The delicious friction of his velvety skin against my silky wetness made me gasp. The suddenness of it was rough and almost too much. I clutched his shoulders while he pounded into me with short, hard thrusts. As my climax burned through my womb and down to my toes, I whimpered. He placed a hand over my mouth to silence my cries and followed after me with a jerk and a shudder.

Slowly, he lowered his hand from my mouth and replaced it with his lips. My head spun at the taste of his tongue, searching and dancing with mine. More footsteps tapped down the hallway. We pulled apart. He tied off the condom and shoved it into his pocket. I tugged my skirt down. He dropped a light kiss on my mouth. This tiny parting gift cracked the concrete wall around my emotions. I searched his eyes, looking for clues, desperate to know his thoughts. His eyes were dark and turbulent, filled with a mixture of anger and resignation, but the gold flecks were back.

Slowly, he smoothed my hair from my face and leaned forward. His breath scalded my ear in a whisper. "You go first. I'm going to slip out the back."

He opened the door and peeked out. At his nod, I went straight into the restroom. With shaking hands, I splashed water on my face and tidied my hair. I stared at the mirror. My reflection stared back at me, a wild-eyed girl with flushed cheeks and a love bite on her neck.

On impulse, I pulled the blond wig from my purse and tugged it over my hair, needing to be someone else, wanting to hide from who I was and what I'd just done. Jo Hollander didn't screw random guys in closets or on the hood of a car. She was quiet and responsible and boring. I ran through the events of the past fifteen minutes, but left the restroom more bewildered than when I'd entered. His delectable hotness had disintegrated my self-control. My thighs burned, and the space between my legs pulsed as I walked out of the diner. Inch by excruciating inch, Carter Eckhouse was burrowing beneath my skin.

CHAPTER 13
CARTER

D arcy's call arrived as I pushed through the back exit of the building, leaving Jo behind in the restroom, hating myself for my weakness. I drew a shaking hand through my hair from forehead to nape. What the fuck was wrong with me? One minute I was sitting next to Jo, smelling her sweet cotton candy scent, and the next minute I was in a broom closet buried balls deep inside her. I scratched my beard. Now, I'd gone and broken my cardinal rule *again*: no repeats.

I let Darcy's call go to voicemail. I needed a moment to pull myself together because, obviously, I was all kinds of messed up. The scent of sex followed me to the parking lot, Jo's perfume clinging to my clothes. Part of me wanted to march back into the diner and take her again, make her cry my name loud enough for everyone to hear. The other part—the dark, fucked-up part—wanted to get in the car and drive until this restless, uneasy, relentless need disappeared. Fuck, fuck, *fuck*. Darcy, always persistent, called back immediately.

"What?" I barked, unleashing my frustrations on her.

"Don't yell at me for doing my job," she shouted back. We'd both been on edge for the past couple of days. While I'd been busy daydreaming about Jo, I'd let a forty-thousand-dollar bond slip through my fingers, and she'd yet to forgive me for it. "One of us has to hold this place together, and apparently that person isn't you."

"Sorry. What's up?" I leaned against the door of the Escalade, gulping in cool air, and waited for her to continue. The lingering haze of orgasm continued to cloud and confuse my thoughts.

"You're being a dick, that's what's up. I'm sick and tired of your grumpy attitude. Whatever is going on with you, you need to stop taking it out on me."

Her words stunned me. Had I really been that bad? "I'm sorry. Really. You're doing a great job."

"Damn straight I am," she said. "And?"

"And I appreciate everything you do. You're the best, and I'm grateful. I don't know why you put up with me."

"Thank you." The tension in her voice eased. We both exhaled in relief. Our squabbles were few and far between, but Darcy never withheld her opinions when my behavior got out of line.

"You're welcome." With thumb and forefinger, I gripped my forehead, squeezing my eyes shut, and tried to focus. "What's up?"

"Taggart called. He needs a favor. He's got a bond on a girl here. I guess she missed her court date or something. His wife is in the hospital and he doesn't have time to track her down. He said it should be straightforward. She doesn't have any priors or anything."

"Give it to Baker." Usually, nothing got my blood pumping like a new case, but not this time, and not a boring one. The easy ones went to the other guys. I reserved my time for the high-dollar, high-profile cases, or ones of special interest. Instead of working, I had the overwhelming desire to go home, sit in front of the TV in my underwear, and drink beer like Mr. H.

"Baker is in Spain, working on an international case. You know that." The clacking of computer keys resumed in the background.

"What about Clyde?"

"He's having his appendix out today. We went over all this yesterday and again this morning." Darcy's exasperated sigh transferred loud and clear through the phone. "What is your deal? Are you okay?"

"I'm fine. Just...I've got some shit on my mind."

"Girl problems?" Even though she was teasing, her question scraped over my raw nerves.

"No."

"Carter, seriously, I'm worried about you. Have you thought about taking some time off? You've been acting weird all week. If I didn't know better, I'd think you were in love or something." We both laughed at the absurdity of the idea; my laughter was hollow, hers genuine. Her tone turned motherly, soothing. "You've been working too hard. Maybe you should take a vacation. When's the last time you got out of town?"

"I don't know. A while, I guess." Although Darcy's suggestion made sense, it would take more than a vacation to get Jo out of my head. The best option was to throw myself into work, hit the bars later tonight, and find someone new to fill my thoughts and my bed. Except, I didn't want anyone else. I wanted Jo. All of her. Stripped naked and writhing on my bed. And just like that, my dick stiffened—again. I'd been walking around semi-hard since the garage sex, and the constant arousal had me on edge. I got in the Escalade and slammed the door shut. "Fuck."

"Excuse me?" Darcy asked. I could picture her eyebrows lifting higher.

"Not you. Sorry." With a heavy sigh, I pulled my faculties together. "Have you sent the email yet? I don't see it."

"It's sending now. Do you want me to book a flight to Rio for you? Or Mexico?" Darcy asked. "A long weekend on the beach might do you some good."

"No. Thanks, but no. Not yet." My inbox pinged as the email came through. "Okay. Got it. I'll look it over and give you a call back if I need anything."

I clicked on the envelope icon and opened the attachment. I

stared at the picture and blinked, unable to believe my eyes. The girl in question was none other than Josephine Hollander.

A t the office, I stormed past Darcy and slammed the door behind me. This was bad, so bad I couldn't find enough profanity to express my feelings. I went straight to the window and glared into a gray sky heavy with rain.

Usually, the boats and clear blue water of the canal calmed my nerves. I'd chosen this office building with strategic care, investing a portion of my trust fund in the prime real estate of downtown Laurel Falls. The twelve-story building was centrally located, across from the courthouse and jail, with an impressive view of the canal from my patio. The upper floors were leased to legal firms and collection agencies. The ground floor held an upscale restaurant and nightclub. Their collective rents provided enough income for me to live out the rest of my life in luxury.

Behind me, the door opened and closed. "What. The. Fuck?" Darcy asked, enunciating each word with sharp precision. "You knocked the picture off the wall with your door slamming."

"Did I?"

The frown slipped from her mouth. In a few short strides, she was at my side, placing a hand on my shoulder. "What's going on? Talk to me."

"That case you sent me—the girl who missed her court date —it's Jo."

Her brow furrowed in confusion. "You mean the coffee shop girl?" I nodded. "So what? It should be easy to pick her up then, right?" My gut twisted at the thought of Jo in jail. The hard glare of Darcy's gaze softened as she read my face. "Oh."

CHAPTER 14

JO

By the time I reached home, the sun hovered on the horizon, casting long shadows across the yard. I should have been home hours ago, but I just couldn't face the thought of sitting at the house, watching reality TV with Dad. Even though I loved him, I needed a few hours to myself, to clear my head and sort through whatever I was feeling for Carter—because I *was* feeling something.

My thighs ached, more from sex than walking the city. The skin of my chin burned from the scrape of Carter's beard, and my lips felt swollen from his kisses. After unlocking the front door, I pressed two fingers against my mouth. No one had ever kissed me like that before, like he was going to die if I didn't kiss him back. The memory made my pulse race.

The house was quiet, still, and dark except for the blue glow of the television from the living room. "Dad?" I flipped the switch in the hall and blinked against the light. "Where are you?"

Silence answered my question. I crept forward, my heart racing for a new and different reason. At the edge of the living room, I paused, letting my eyes adjust to the dimness. Dad's silhouette emerged from the gloom. He was slumped over in his chair. I ran to his side, mouth dry, stomach twisting then breathed a sigh of relief to see his chest rising and falling.

"Dad?" I shook his shoulder, and he grunted. "Wake up."

Judging by the stench of his breath and the scattered empty beer cans, he was drunk. Anger clutched my chest, squeezing my lungs until I wanted to scream. Then I saw the box of photographs in his lap, the pictures of Mom, of better days, when life held promise and laughter. I shook his shoulder again, this time with kindness. Although my father drank quite often, I'd only seen him truly drunk once before, the day after Mom had died.

"Julie?" He blinked up at me, brow furrowed in confusion, and my heart squeezed at the sound of my mom's name.

"No, Dad. It's me. Jo." I withdrew the box from beneath his limp arm and set it aside.

"Jo? Where have you been all day?" Reality slowly dawned in his eyes. With it returned the pain and anguish he usually hid from me.

"I went for a walk."

"That was a long damn walk," he said, shoving upright in the chair. "I could have starved to death."

"The last I checked, you're a grown man and perfectly capable of fixing your own meals," I snapped. Since Mom had died, the frustration and resentment had been welling inside me. I'd bottled it up for so long that once it found a fissure to escape, it burst out of me like the cork from a champagne bottle. "Why is everything my responsibility? I'm sick of being the only person around here holding things together. It's not my job to run the coffee shop. It's not my job to take care of you. I'm not Mom. I'm not your wife."

The words hung in the air between us, laced with the painful truth. I didn't want to hurt him, but I just couldn't keep up the charade any longer. My soul ached to be free from obligations that weren't mine to uphold.

"Jo, I'm—" Dad began, but I stopped him with a wave of my hand.

"No. I don't want to hear it." My footsteps thundered down the hall and up the stairs to the bedroom. I slammed the door so hard that the entire house shuddered. Part of me felt horrible for talking to my father that way, a man I used to respect and admire. Another part of me seethed with anger. When Mom had died, she'd left all of us, not just him, but I'd never been allowed to grieve. I had to be the one to pick up the pieces and hold the family together.

My vision blurred with tears. I stalked around the tiny bedroom, slamming doors and drawers, overcome with the need to scream. Instead, I threw my toothbrush and a nightshirt into a tote bag. I had to get out of here. One more minute within the confines of this prison, and I was going to lose my freaking mind.

"Where are you going?" Dad met me at the bottom of the stairs on wobbly legs, his face pale.

"Out," I said. In truth, I had no idea where I was going. I didn't care. I just had to get away.

CHAPTER 15

CARTER

Darcy stared at me with round eyes, Jo's case file spread across the desk between us. "What are you going to do?"

"I don't know. Bring her in, I guess." The thought turned my blood to ice. Sweet, sunny Jo didn't belong behind the concrete walls of a jail cell. The coldhearted bastard inside me sat like a devil upon my shoulder, whispering in my ear. Jo was an easy capture. I could swing by her house, pick her up, drop her off at the jail, and be home before bedtime. She'd hate me with a passion afterward. If I wanted to sever the ties between us, a night in jail should do the trick. On the other hand, the softness of her lips haunted me, the sound of her sweet kitten moans when I drove into her, the way her nails dug into my shoulders when she came, the light in her eyes whenever I said something funny. This feeling, this unrest, compared to nothing else in my experience, and it all centered around her.

"The preliminary hearing was today, and it looks like the hearing has been rescheduled for next week, providing the defendant is caught." The papers whirred as she rifled through the file. "There's also a civil suit requesting a boatload of monetary damages." Her exhaled breath ruffled the fringe of her bangs. "Somebody is really pissed at her."

"Yep, well—" My feet felt like two-ton weights as I trudged toward the door. "Might as well get this over."

"You're seriously going to haul this girl in?" Darcy blocked the doorway, spreading her hands against the frame.

"If I don't do it, someone else will, Taggart will be out his money, and I'll lose face." The contents of my stomach churned.

"Sometimes you're so frustrating. Your ginormous ego isn't the most important thing in the world." She crossed her arms over her chest, shaking her head until the dangly earrings jangled. "There's obviously more to this story than meets the eye. Let me do a little investigating and see what I can find out. In the meantime, go find this girl and talk to her, Carter."

Apparently, Darcy had lost her mind. I stared at her, trying to work through her words. "Are you suggesting that I sit on this? You know I can't do that."

"No, I'm suggesting you hear her side of the story before you throw her to the wolves. I mean, obviously, you have feelings for her." She stifled a chuckle then cleared her throat. "I mean, you're *friends*, right? Give her an opportunity to clear things up first." I nodded, some of the panic subsiding in my chest. "This might be a simple misunderstanding."

"Okay. Makes sense." Heat burned my face. I avoided her gaze, gathering up the paperwork. "Call Taggart and stall for me. I'll go over to her house and see if I can sort this out."

At least, that had been the plan. Halfway to the Hollander house, I had a change of heart. During my stint in the Marines, I'd stared down the barrel of an enemy rifle more times than I could count, but the idea of facing Jo's disappointment turned this Purple Heart recipient into a sniveling coward. In that moment, I hated her for making me question everything I knew about women and relationships. I hated myself more for being unable to resist her, for caring more about her welfare than the business I'd struggled and sacrificed to build.

While I waited for the stoplight to change from red to green, I drummed my fingers on the steering wheel. I'd never forfeited a bond by choice. Never. Not once. It was one of the reasons I excelled in my field. I'd built a reputation of being ruthless and relentless and unforgiving. Benson and Clyde often joked that I'd turn in my own mother if it came down to it.

Raindrops splattered on the windshield. From the corner of my eye, I caught the flash of blond hair. Jo crossed the street in front of me, heading toward the bus stop, head down, hands shoved into the pockets of her sweater. If she was wearing the wig, she must be intending to stalk her ex-fiancé. I punched the steering wheel. A few hours ago, we'd had the best sex of my life, and now she was obsessing over some other guy. The thought should have thrilled me. No strings. No expectations. Just the way I liked it. I could take her into the jail with a clear conscience. But I didn't like the idea of her wanting someone else. Especially someone who'd treated her so badly. The situation echoed my mother's life too closely. My temper simmered. Conflict burned inside my chest.

The car behind me honked its horn. Sometime during my musings, the stoplight had changed colors. I hit the gas, tires squealing, and raced through the intersection. *I don't care. I don't care. I. Do. Not. Care.* But I did care—more than I wanted. What if, by some circumstance, she ran into this douchebag? What if he took her back? He'd be crazy not to want her. The notion turned my stomach. She was too sweet and too nice to end up like my mom. Even worse, some other bounty hunter might pick her up. How could I trust her care to the callous hands of a stranger?

I circled the block and came up beside her. I lowered the window on the passenger side. "Hey, you want a ride?"

She glanced over her shoulder, startled, like someone might see us. "Um, okay. Sure."

I leaned across the seat to open the door for her. She hopped in.

Her short skirt rode up her legs, offering a flash of trim thighs, the thighs I'd been between earlier. My dick stirred to life. I'd been inside her a short time ago, but I wanted her again. I wanted more. Twice wasn't enough, and I had sneaking suspicion that three times wouldn't be enough either.

"Going stalking, are we?" Despite my best efforts, I couldn't curb the jealousy in my tone.

"No." She pulled the wig off and fluffed her hair with her fingers. "I just— The rain— I thought—" Her words stopped abruptly.

"It's getting ready to storm. You should be home." To keep from betraying my thoughts to her, I stared straight ahead, concentrating on the road. If I looked at her, she'd be able to see the jealousy and turmoil tormenting me.

"No. I'm not going back there. Not tonight." The urgency in her voice brought me up short. "You can drop me at the Winthrop Hotel."

The Winthrop was a seedy, second-class establishment famous for clandestine affairs and drug deals gone wrong. I'd captured more than my fair share of fugitives in its dingy halls. The bar on the ground floor had proved an excellent place to pick up a one-night stand. I exhaled, thinking of all the reasons I should keep my mouth shut and all the reason I shouldn't. The exit to the jail approached with frightening swiftness. I needed to make a decision and fast.

"Why the Winthrop?" With great effort, I kept my tone neutral, disinterested. "Do you go there often?" A new and disturbing thought took root. Maybe she was meeting someone there. My heart skipped a beat.

"Don't worry about it." She wrapped her arms around her waist and squeezed, like she was hugging herself. "I'll be fine. I just need to get away from home for a bit."

Just a few more blocks, Carter, and you can be rid of her. I made the turn to the jail. Its beige limestone façade loomed in the distance, menacing and absolute. No more second guessing myself. No more late-night phone sex. No more cotton candy perfume. And no more chances of losing my mind over a girl who shouldn't matter.

Three blocks. Two blocks. One block. My hand trembled as I signaled to make the turn into the jail parking garage. This was it. Now or never. Cold sweat beaded on my forehead. Did I want to be that guy? The one who took a sweet, hardworking girl to jail for something she may or may not have done? If I did, I'd never be able to look at myself in the mirror. How would I face Rhett and Bronte? Her father? Finally, my good conscience won the war. The entrance to the jail came and went. I kept driving.

J o wrinkled her nose when she opened the door to her hotel suite. Dingy yellow walls, red shag carpet, and street noise filled the room. Despite the outdated décor, the scents of laundry detergent and cleaners offered hope. After a sigh of resignation, she yanked the cover off the bed and tossed it aside.

"You never what's on those things. Have you seen the TV shows where they use the black light?" A shiver wracked her petite frame. "It's disgusting what they find."

"Yeah." I shoved my hands in my pockets, painfully aware of the number of times I'd had sex on random hotel bedspreads. From my perspective, this hotel ranked one step above the jail. It was fine for a hookup but not for a respectable girl like Jo. "Come on. Let me take you home."

"No." The finality of her denial reverberated in the air between us. "I'll be fine for one night."

"Okay, well, guess I'll take off then." I needed to retreat, to deconstruct my motivations for letting her off the hook. Despite my intentions, my feet stuck to the floor, immoveable.

"You don't have to go." The unfamiliar glint in her eyes sent my heart into arrhythmia. "Please."

Thump. The wall shook from the force of an impact on the other side. *Thump, thump.* Jo and I flinched. The framed landscape above the dresser vibrated. A high-pitched moan, female in origin, carried through the plaster. *Thump, thump, thump.*

"That's right. Take it, baby," a man's voice growled. *Thump. Thump.* "Do you like that?"

Jo's lips quivered. She drew her bottom lip between her teeth. An adorable shade of pink lit up her cheeks. Mirth sparked in her blue eyes. "Oh my God."

"Somebody's having a good time." My mouth twitched as I tried to hold back the laughter. "You could ask for a different room."

"No. It's fine. I'll turn on the TV." Her gaze dipped to my mouth and held. Fuck my heart. It skittered against my ribs, my erratic pulse drowning out the thud of the headboard next door. She took a step toward me. "Or maybe we could show them how it's done."

"I'm not so sure that's a good idea." Another step closer, and my mouth went dry.

"Why not? We've never done it in a bed." The next step brought her within inches. I swallowed and stared down at her, my body on high alert at her proximity. "You don't like having sex with me?"

"You know damn good and well that I like it." To prove the point, my blood raced to my crotch, leaving me lightheaded. "But we were supposed to be a one-time thing."

"But not good enough for another encore?" One of her hands landed on my chest and slid slowly over my sternum. She hooked a finger in the waistband of my jeans and jerked my pelvis against hers. "Do you want more?"

If I'd been a better man, I would have pushed her away, but the sight of those baby blues blinking up at me through long lashes wrecked my good intentions. "Yes."

With her gaze still locked on my mouth, her fingers found my belt buckle, unfastened it. The leather hissed through the belt loops as she yanked it free. "You know what I like about you, Carter?"

"For the life of me, I have no idea," I said, unable to think with her touch whispering over my fly.

"You don't want anything in return. It's just sex for you. Uncomplicated. No strings. No lies between us."

Guilt mingled with arousal. I needed to tell her. "Jo, I—"

She stopped me with a press of her fingertip to my lips. "Don't. Whatever it is, don't say it. Not right now. I just need you to make me forget all the ways my life sucks." As she spoke, she edged her small hand into my pants and wrapped it around my shaft. "Let's pretend we're two strangers, fucking for the first time." The soft fullness of her mouth pressed above the notch in my collarbone. Her breath burned down the front of my T-shirt, moving lower as she knelt in front of me. "You can do that, can't you, Carter?"

I wanted to answer, but her lips enveloped the swollen crown of my dick. The heat and wetness and velvety smoothness of her mouth erased every excuse in my head. With a hand around my base, she took me in, all the way to the root. Instead of replying, I groaned and fisted a hand in her hair to guide her mouth. My tip hit the back of her throat. When she swallowed, the convulsing of her muscles made me shudder. Nothing had ever felt this good, this perfect, this amazing. I fought against the urge to take her face between my hands and thrust. She pulled back, letting go with a *pop*.

"Do we have an agreement?" she asked. "Or do you want me to stop?"

"Hell no, I don't want you to stop." The sight of her on her knees in front of me, my erection bobbing between us, glistening from her mouth, obliterated the last of my misgivings. With both hands on her biceps, I hauled her to her feet and crushed my mouth against hers, powerless to stop myself. The attraction between us was too strong. I surrendered to it, teasing her tongue with mine, savoring her. She tasted of toothpaste and bubble gum. When we broke apart, blind need broke the last of my self-control. I picked her up and tossed her onto the bed. "Take off your clothes." My voice was harsh and raspy. "I'm going to give the guy next door a run for his money."

CHAPTER 16
CARTER

With my rules broken and my pants around my ankles, I tossed caution to the wind. Jo writhed and moaned beneath me, meeting each pump of my hips with a soft grunt. Her sounds made me wild. The smoothness of her skin, the vise of her legs around my waist, and the squeak of bedsprings filled my senses.

When this was over, I'd deal with the consequences, but for now, all I could think about was quenching the unending thirst for her body. I swallowed her moans with my kisses, devoured her lips and tongue, claimed her tight pussy. Her nails dug into my back, scraping over the skin, clawing and raking. I brought her to climax twice before I allowed myself to come, and once we'd caught our breath, we began again.

When dawn glowed behind the closed drapes, we collapsed next to each other in a mess of tangled bedsheets. Jo groaned and stretched lazily, her tits jiggling from the movement, nipples still tight. I turned on my side to face her, propping up on an elbow, and drew a fingertip down the creamy stretch of skin between her breasts and navel. With a giggle, she caught my large finger in her small hand.

"Don't. I'm ticklish."

"Are you?" To test the statement, I poked her in the ribs. She doubled up, face bright red from sex and repressed laughter. The sound lodged in my chest, somewhere around the vicinity of my heart.

"Yes. Stop it."

"And what if I don't?" I challenged her with my gaze. An unbearable lightness expanded inside me. I hadn't felt this happy or carefree since—well, ever.

"Then I'll have to teach you a lesson." In one smooth motion, she straddled my hips and pinned my wrists at my sides. I could have broken her hold without effort, but I didn't want to escape. In fact, I liked it when she got feisty and took control. I bucked, pretending to struggle, rewarded by more of her laughter and smiles. She slapped my thigh. "Behave."

"You behave." I rolled her beneath me, stretching out on top of her, enjoying the glide of my hairy legs against her smooth, bare skin.

"Where's the fun in that?" Her voice softened, eyes going hazy as her sex rubbed against my stirring cock.

I kissed her again, long and slow and deep, with the intent of stealing everything she offered to me. The last time I'd made out had been in junior high school with Melissa Martin. Afterward, Melissa had gone straight to the bleachers and made out with one of my classmates. I'd forgiven her because she'd taught me some mad skills, skills that had come in handy when my voice had changed and I'd shot up another six inches in height, skills I put to use with Jo. In fact, that was the last time a girl had given me this strange euphoria. The galloping organ in my chest bounced between my ribs. In the back of my mind, I knew this bliss had to end, probably sooner than later, and I meant to make the most of every precious second.

"Carter, wait." Jo squirmed. I pulled back, admiring the flush of her cheeks and her red, swollen lips. "I need to go to the bathroom."

"Alright, hurry back." I gave her a little slap on the ass. She smiled at me over her shoulder and sashayed naked to the bathroom.

There was nothing I loved more than a confident girl, one who didn't cling to the bedsheets or hide her body. In my opinion, all women were beautiful in their own way, and I'd never been one to discriminate according to age or weight.

I rolled onto my back, clasped my hands behind my head, and stared at the water stain on the ceiling. My muscles ached in all the right places. For the first time in my life, I didn't want to sprint out the door, making lame excuses, anxious to move on. I was content to lie there, eager to find out what came next. Maybe it was time to give this monogamy concept a chance. Rhett seemed to think highly of it. I was bumbling into uncharted territory, having never had a girlfriend, but Jo seemed like the perfect choice.

"I think we should start seeing each other," I said, my voice too high and thin, breaking like a teenage boy.

"What's this?" Jo asked, her voice strange.

We spoke in unison, our words colliding and smashing into each other.

The ominous tone of her voice sparked confusion. I rolled onto my side, the smile sliding from my face. In her hands, she held the arrest warrant. It must have fallen out of my pocket when we'd torn off our clothing. The bottom dropped out of my stomach. Her face went pale. I jumped out of bed, intending to—I didn't know what I was intending to do—but I couldn't lay there with her staring at me like a doe in the crosshairs of a hunter's rifle.

"Carter, start talking. Right now."

"I can explain," I said, my panic growing.

"Wait a second." She placed a hand in the air between us, palm facing outward, a scowl darkening her face. "Please tell me that you did not just ask me to be your girlfriend minutes before you planned on taking me to jail."

"I— You— We—" My tongue felt too big and too thick to form sentences.

She closed her hand into a fist then pointed an index finger into the air. "Just to be clear, when you picked me up last night, did you intend to take me in? Is that what you were doing, hunting me down?" The pieces fell into place as shown by the disappointment in her eyes. "That's why you drove by the jail. Then you must have decided on one last screw before turning me over." Her nostrils flared. "How very Carter of you."

"Yes. I mean, no. No." When she said it like that, I sounded like a huge asshole. "Fu-u-uck," I growled. Each passing minute drew me further and further into a place I didn't care to be. "I meant what I said. I think we should go out. It has nothing to do with the warrant."

"Are you kidding me? How could you do this? You're such a dick." She grabbed the nearest item, a bar of hotel soap, and chucked it at me. I became painfully aware that I was naked and my family jewels were under real threat of attack. Using a pillow as a shield, I covered my junk and took a step toward her. Her chin quivered, indignation darkening her blue eyes to navy. "Don't you dare touch me."

"What was I supposed to do? You missed your court date. Your bondsman called me to pick you up and take you in, but I haven't— I'm not." The excuses tumbled over each other while I tried to string together two coherent thoughts.

"I'm not going to jail." She stared at the warrant, brows furrowed in confusion. "I didn't know anything about a court date. This can't be right."

"That's what they all say." I'd heard this story a million times. The unrest rekindled in my veins. She had every right to be pissed, and now I was angry too, because she was lying to me. "How could you not know? Breaking and entering, harassment, and a restraining order. Those are some very impressive crimes, young lady. Now that you've missed your court date, you're looking at jail time for sure."

"I'm telling you, I didn't know anything about a court date." With her eyes downcast, she skimmed over the warrant. "The address on here, it's my old address, Harold's address."

At the mention of her ex-fiancé's name, an uncomfortable fire ignited in my veins. Was she still hung up on him? The pain of rejection combined with jealousy. My voice came out louder and angrier than I intended. "Give me one good reason why I shouldn't take you straight to jail."

"Don't yell at me." Chin quivering, she raised her eyes to mine, eyes blazing with frustration.

"I'm not yelling." I sank to the edge of the mattress, feeling weak. "Why did you do all these things? I can't decide if you're crazy, a criminal, or just unlucky."

She shook her head, lips pressing into a tight white line. "You're calling *me* insane? Seriously? You came up to my room under false pretenses, shagged me within an inch of my life, ask me to be your girlfriend, then counter the offer with a trip to the Laurel County lockup. What the hell?"

"Talk to me, Jo. I'm not taking you anywhere until I hear your side of the story. Why did you do all those things? Are you still in love with the guy?" An unfamiliar squeeze clutched my chest. If she said yes, I was going to punch something. I knew this story, my mother's story. She clung to my father, going above and beyond reason to keep him in her life, using whatever means necessary.

"He has my dog," she said in a tiny, quiet voice.

I thought she was kidding until I caught the glimmer of tears in her eyes. "For real? You went to jail over a dog?"

"Yes. He was mine long before Harold and I moved in together." She closed her eyes, like she was gathering her strength. "When we broke up, he threw me out, wouldn't let me have my things, and told all the neighbors that I wasn't allowed back. I was furious about the way he'd ended things, and then to steal my dog...it was so unfair. I waited until he left for work and went into the apartment to take Zipper and my stuff. One of the neighbors saw me and called the cops. Harold, being the dick that he is, pressed charges. It wasn't enough for him to hurt me. He had to humiliate me with a restraining order on top of it."

"What a fucker," I said, more to myself than to her. "Why don't you take him to court?"

"He's got some powerful friends." She lifted an eyebrow. "I don't have enough money or connections to fight him."

The dejected curve of her mouth twisted my heart. I pulled her onto my lap and ran a finger down the slope of her cheek. "You're in some deep shit." The warmth of her small body melted the ice I'd been carrying around my heart and awakened a primitive need to protect her. I pressed a kiss to the top of her head, not caring that the last of my rules had been obliterated. "You need to turn yourself in ASAP."

"I can't." She pushed away, turning terrified eyes to mine. "Please, Carter. I'm begging you. If I go to jail, who will run the coffee shop? Dad will lose everything. We're already in financial trouble."

"It's only a matter of time until someone picks you up. You're just lucky the guy who wrote your bond is a friend of mine. I might be able to stall for a little while but not indefinitely." Her lower lip trembled. I ran the pad of my thumb across it, wanting to make her smile again. "Let me make a few calls. I know people. I might be able to help. In the meantime, you should lay low. No more stalking. Stay away from your house. That's the first place they'll look. Understand?"

She nodded. Before I could stop myself, I put my lips to hers. For once, my intentions weren't sexual, although the desire remained. This kiss was filled with the need to protect and soothe the both of us.

"What about work? I have to be there. Lyle is covering for me this morning, but I've got to check in on him."

"No." I shook my head.

"But—"

"You can't risk it." I took her chin in my fingers and tilted her face to mine. The faith in her eyes broke me in a thousand different ways. No one had ever looked at me with such blind trust. She knew my womanizing ways, my inability to form relationships, my flaws—hell, I'd fucked her in a diner and had walked away without a word—yet, she still believed in me. "Lyle can take over. Rhett and Bronte will help. And what about your dad? I'm sure he'll pitch in."

"I can't tell him. He's going to be so disappointed." A tear dropped from her chin and landed on our clasped hands. "I've made such a mess of things. I just wanted to get my dog back, to have that one thing for myself."

"Your dad will understand. We'll tell him together." I straightened, rising to the challenge. I'd make this work or die trying. It was what I did best—solve problems. Usually, they were of my own making, but this would be a good change of pace.

CHAPTER 17

JO

The Escalade hummed smoothly through my neighborhood. Since leaving the hotel, I'd remained silent. In all my life, I'd never been so embarrassed. If I'd known about the court date, I would have made every effort to appear. For Carter, of all people, to haul me in—well, it was beyond demeaning. The humiliation prevented me from looking directly at him or speaking. Instead, I peered at his profile through my peripheral vision. He stared down the road, one hand resting on top of the steering wheel, the other rubbing his forehead like he had a headache.

Well, served him right. I had both a headache and a pain in my ass. *Him*. In the space of twenty-four hours, he'd managed to give me a record-breaking number of orgasms, followed by the threat of incarceration, and an offer to be his girlfriend. His inconsistency confused and irritated me. For now, my worries centered around the missed court appearance. I'd spent a few hours in jail for the initial charges, and it had been long enough for me to decide a repeat visit could never happen. This girl wasn't cut out for prison life.

The refrain of AC/DC's "Highway to Hell" blasted from his phone, resting in the console. He hit the Bluetooth button on the steering wheel. "Hey, Darcy. What's the good news? You're on speak-erphone, and Jo is in the car. Keep it clean."

A brash female voice with a decidedly New Jersey accent blasted from the speakers. "I resent that. I'm always professional." Carter winced and dialed down the volume a notch. "I got hold of Calloway. He can see you tomorrow morning. That's the good news. The bad news is that Taggart also contacted a few other bounty hunters on this case, so you're not the only one looking for her."

"Shit," Carter muttered. "You didn't tell him about the situation, did you?"

Her voice carried a wounded tone. "Of course not. This isn't my first rodeo, Carter."

"I know. I just wanted to see what we're dealing with." He drummed his fingers on the steering wheel. "Thanks for the help."

"You're welcome. Oh, and I'm supposed to remind you about the wedding this weekend."

"Great." Carter growled and shoved a hand through his long, flowing locks. "I forgot all about it."

"Of course you did. That's why you need me." Laughter laced her voice, accompanied by an incessant jingling, like the clinking of heavy jewelry. "I had your tux cleaned. I hung it in your bedroom closet. Don't forget to get a haircut and shave off that rat's nest on your face."

The intimacy of her words sent a prickle of jealousy up my back. He'd never mentioned Darcy before, but from the ease of their conversation, they were well acquainted. Not only did she possess a key to his apartment, she'd been in his bedroom. I huffed and turned my gaze back to the window. Whatever he and Darcy did behind closed doors was none of my business, but no matter how many times I told myself that, I couldn't shake the jealousy.

Carter flushed, his fingers going to the hair on his chin. "Don't be a hater, Darcy."

Their conversation turned to other business, allowing my mind to drift. The number of problems in my life continued to mount. The coffee shop needed more staff. Last month's rent had yet to be paid. Harold had my dog, and I was now a fugitive from the law in the possession of a bounty hunter who both thrilled and annoyed me. I couldn't stop thinking about the way he'd kissed me this morning, long and deep and lingering. No one had ever kissed me like that. My lips felt bruised and swollen, the space between my legs throbbed in the best possible way, and every muscle in my body ached, like I'd been torn apart and put back together.

Once we reached the house, Carter sent me upstairs. "Go clean up. I'm going to talk to Mr. H and make a few phone calls."

The solitude of my bathroom offered little comfort beyond familiarity. Everything was in the same place, same purple towels, same Cotton Candy Delight shower gel and body lotion on the shelf. I'd been gone less than a day, but my life had taken a new and unwelcome turn. The bathroom was the same, but I had changed. I could hardly look at myself in the mirror. Over the years, I'd done some dumb things, smoked pot in the restroom at high school, been suspended for skipping class, but I'd never been arrested. Dad was going to be so disappointed. After the hurtful things I'd said last night, he would never forgive me, and I couldn't blame him.

With a heavy heart, I showered and took my sweet time about it. When I'd stalled as long as possible, I trudged downstairs to face the consequences, butterflies in my stomach. Dad greeted me with open arms, pulled me into a hug, and squeezed me tight. Hot tears burned my eyes. I blinked them back. I didn't deserve his compassion or understanding. I wanted him to yell and threaten and punish me for being an idiot.

"I'm so sorry," he said over and over into my hair. "I let you take on all the responsibility, and that's not what a father does. I've been so busy feeling sorry for myself that I forgot to take care of you."

"It's okay, Dad." I tried to loosen his grip, but he only held me tighter. Over his shoulder, I saw Carter talking on his phone, pacing back and forth down the hallway. "I'm an adult. I don't need you to take care of me."

"No, it's not okay. I've been selfish. You've given up your life to hold things together. I never worried about you the way I worried about Bronte. You've always been the strong one, the responsible one." He smoothed my hair back from my face. The strength in his arms reminded me of the dad I used to know, the one who'd kissed my skinned knees and always made everything better. "That doesn't excuse what you've done. You'll have to answer for it, but I'll do whatever it takes to help you."

A tremor threatened my control. I bit my lower lip. *I will not cry. I. Will. Not. Cry.* I didn't know what Carter had said, but somehow he'd managed to soothe my father's temper and turn a disaster into a manageable event. Our eyes met across the faded pink rug. He winked, and a different kind of warmth traveled into my core. This was more than sexual attraction; it was confusing and exhilarating and frightening.

From the back of the house, the screen door creaked and slammed. Bronte and Rhett entered through the kitchen, their faces grim. My sister charged at me like a bull in front of a waving red cape.

I shot Carter an exasperated look. "You didn't waste any time spreading the good news, did you?"

"Simmer down. They need to know what's going on," he said. The jumping muscle beneath his cheekbone gave him a menacing appearance.

"We're here to lend a hand any way we can," Rhett said. "Family sticks together."

Bronte's blue eyes watered with sympathy and guilt. "I wish you'd told me. You can always talk to me, you know?"

"I know." The words caught on the lump in my throat. When she pulled me into a tight hug, the lump grew larger. I held on to her, my anxiety easing under her embrace. Although we fought like cats and dogs, she'd always been my best friend. Looking at the circle of support around me, I gained new perspective on my life. I'd been so busy hating on Harold that I'd overlooked all the blessings that had come from our breakup. I loved the coffee shop, meeting new customers, the joy in serving the perfect cup of cappuccino to someone in need of a smile. Those things would never have come about if I'd stayed with Harold. Maybe I needed to be grateful for what I had instead of pining for what I'd lost.

"Rhett and I will help take care of things until you get back," Bronte said. She drew away then thumped me across the back of the head with her hand.

"Ouch." I scowled and rubbed my crown. "What was that for?"

"That's for being a dipshit. Don't ever do that again."

Everyone stared then burst into laughter, including me. After the stress of the morning, it felt good to release the emotions on something other than tears. That was when her words hit home. I narrowed my eyes suspiciously. "What do you mean, when I get back?"

"You're coming to stay with me for a few days." Carter strode toward me. The lines of his body crackled with electricity. He pocketed his phone. His gaze cut through me and into me and devoured me. I felt naked and vulnerable. "No one will think to look for you at my place." The tense line of his jaw softened, setting into motion all the fluttery attraction I'd been fighting against. "Pack a bag, and we'll get out of here."

Given Carter's bachelor status, I'd never devoted much thought to his residence. I'd assumed he had an apartment littered with empty pizza boxes and crushed beer cans. Then again, up to this point, my assumptions had been wrong about him. Despite his best efforts to hide it from everyone, his recent actions had revealed his true character. Beneath his rough and wild exterior lurked a sympathetic soul and a kind heart.

Through the car window, the quiet neighborhoods evolved into the city's warehouse district. I'd only been here a handful of times, and stared at the unfamiliar streets. Recently, there had been a movement of trendy and upscale businesses to the area, revitalizing what had once been a derelict zone. We passed micro-breweries, restaurants, and converted apartments. Traffic lights reflected off the rain-slicked streets. The windshield wipers beat a comforting tattoo, echoing the rhythm of my poor little heart.

"Home sweet home," he said in a tone I couldn't decipher. We stopped in front of a five-story, brown brick warehouse. The plaque above the foundation read *Hudson Steel Building, Erected 1892*. With the press of a button, the enormous overhead door lifted. He pulled the Escalade through the door and parked in what appeared to be the living room of his apartment. Except it was large enough to be the lobby of The Four Seasons Hotel.

I stared open-mouthed, turning in a circle, dizzy from the sights. Exposed pipes and beams crisscrossed through five stories of open space. Gray daylight illuminated enormous windows and a huge skylight at the very top. To my right, a series of metal stairs led to different levels of lofts and balconies.

Carter said, "Better close your mouth. Something's going to fly in there."

His words broke my trance. "You live here?"

"Yep." With my overnight bag in hand, he strode toward a freight elevator.

"For real? This whole thing is yours?" I trotted after him, feeling foolish and amazed and awestruck. "Who are you—Batman?"

"Well, I own the building. This half is my residence. The other side of the building is loft apartments for rent." His biceps bulged as he slid open the door to the elevator cage.

I swallowed and followed him inside, feeling like I'd fallen down the rabbit hole and landed in an alternate universe. With the throw of a lever and the grinding of gears, the elevator lurched into motion and began to ascend. After a painful silence fraught with unspoken conflict, we arrived at the top floor. The elevator opened into a vestibule with two pairs of double doors. Carter opened the doors to my left. We entered a vast master suite furnished in earthy tones and heavy, masculine furniture.

"You can sleep in here." He tossed my duffel bag on the king-size bed and turned to leave. "I'll take the room next door."

"Carter, I can't take your room. It wouldn't be right. I'll stay in the other room or I can sleep on the sofa." When I touched his arm, he winced, like I'd stung him. Somewhere between the hotel and his house, we'd become intimate strangers. I knew the way his legs trembled right before he came, the quirk of his left eyebrow when I said something amusing, and the star tattoo below his left hipbone. All these things meant nothing now, standing together in his bedroom, with an ocean of misunderstandings and questions between us.

"It's no problem. The other rooms aren't finished, and I want you to be comfortable. Make yourself at home. I insist." He shoved his hands deep into his pockets and kept walking, pausing at the door. "Someone comes in to clean a few days a week. There isn't much to eat. I can order a pizza or something if you're hungry."

"It's okay. You don't need to go to any trouble." My insides quivered with nervous anxiety. Food hovered at the bottom on my list of priorities. After the events of the day, I needed a hot shower and a good cry to get myself back on track.

He shrugged. "It's no big deal."

"It's a big deal to me." I took another step toward him, and he took a step back. The shuttered look had returned to his gaze.

From his jeans pocket, his phone buzzed. He answered the call with a terse, "Yeah?" The unmistakable pitch of a female voice floated in the air. His eyes met mine then flicked away. He went into the next room and closed the door.

I flopped onto the bed and tried to ignore the masculine rumble of his voice through the walls.

Finally, alone, I let the tears flow—tears of relief and guilt and anger and frustration. What the hell was happening? One minute, I controlled my life, and the next minute, I was holed up in Carter's massive bedroom, a fugitive from the law. The thought of jail terrified me. All this trouble because of my inability to let go of a dog.

After a few minutes of self-pity, I dried my tears and gathered the shreds of my dignity. I unpacked my bag and investigated the room. A huge fireplace took up the entire south wall. Buttery leather armchairs faced an enormous flat-screen TV, a coffee table with a chess board, and an old-fashioned pinball machine. It was a beautiful room but lacked personality—no family photos, no personal touches, nothing to show that anyone lived there.

Was this his life? Solitary? Lonely? For the first time, I realized how little I knew of him, of his family, his personal life. This peek into his home added a new layer to his already convoluted personality. I owed him a lot. Maybe he wasn't such a bad guy after all. And he certainly was, without question, the best sex I'd ever had. Once I got through this mess, I wanted to learn more about him.

As if on cue, his bedroom door opened, and he stepped into the hall. He was freshly showered. The scent of his soap drifted across the room, teasing my nose, making me want him. Gold-brown eyes avoided mine.

"I'm going back to work," he said. "I'm not sure what time I'll be home. Late. Don't wait up."

"Okay." I sat on the bed, tucking a foot beneath me. Of course he had things to do, and of course he'd be out late. Everyone knew Carter was a playboy, haunting dive bars, picking up women, partying all night. Just because he'd taken me in didn't mean he'd given up his lifestyle. I tried to curb the disappointment in my voice. "Be careful. Have a nice night."

"Yeah," he said. Inwardly, I rolled my eyes. I sounded like an overprotective mother. His broad shoulders turned and moved toward the elevator.

"Wait." I sprang from the bed and trotted after him. "I really appreciate this—what you're doing for me. I'll find a way to pay you back."

"I don't want your money." He shoved his hands into his pockets.

"But there is something you could do for me."

"Sure. Anything."

"I have a wedding on Saturday, and I need a date."

I stared at him, my overtaxed brain struggling to process his question. "You want me to fix you up with someone?"

"No, dummy." A hint of a smile twitched the left corner of his mouth. "I want *you* to be my date."

"Carter, about your question—about seeing each other—"

He cut me off with a sarcastic smirk. "Yeah, about that. Forget it. I don't know what I was thinking. I'm not that kind of guy, and you obviously have relationship issues." The way he rushed to clarify the situation tweaked my pride, but I couldn't fault his logic. "The wedding and reception are on Saturday. It'll be formal and stuffy and super boring, but I promised...someone...I'd be there."

The last thing I wanted to do was spend time at a stranger's wedding when my own engagement had ended so badly. I studied his face, searching for his motivation. The early afternoon sun fell in dappled spots across the polished pine floor, casting half his face in shadows, sharpening his features. His T-shirt molded to the dips and swells of his muscular torso. He was, without a doubt, a stallion of a man. My fingers curled and uncurled, fighting against the urge to touch him. There must have been dozens of women eager and willing to spend a weekend with him, women who were prettier and sexier than me. Had I missed my chance to lay a claim on him?

"I didn't pack anything for a wedding," I said.

"I'll have Darcy take care of it." His gaze wandered up and down my body. "You're what? A size four?"

"Six," I said.

He nodded and with those parting words, left me standing barefoot, in the middle of his house. At the mention of Darcy's name, my head thumped with a mixture of jealousy and resignation. A man like Carter could never be tamed. He'd never be satisfied with one woman, and the sooner I accepted the fact, the sooner I could get over this all-consuming desire to have him.

CHAPTER 18
CARTER

After work, I went for a few beers at the bar because I couldn't trust myself to be alone with Jo. I waited until she'd be asleep then crept into the apartment. I'd never intended to let my lust get so out of control, but I had to admit the situation had gotten crazy. I didn't do things like this. I didn't bring women into my home. I didn't skirt the law to protect them. Now, with only a wall between us, I couldn't get her out of my head. I fell asleep with my dick in my hand, dreamed of her pretty tits, and awoke with a raging erection and a mild hangover.

The smell of bacon and coffee lured me from the bedroom. Jo stood in front of the stove, wearing one of my oversized T-shirts, her hair piled high on top of her head. Fuck me if it wasn't the sexiest thing I'd ever seen—a woman in my clothes, in my kitchen, cooking food for me. The caveman inside me roared his approval.

"You're wearing my shirt." The outlines of her breasts pressed against the thin cotton. A strange shiver ran down my back as my gaze lowered to the short hemline, the pale skin of her thighs, and her bare feet. Pink polish tipped her toes. Even her feet turned me on.

"Um, yes. I forgot to pack pajamas." One of her small, fragile fingers ran along the inside of the collar, like she was letting off steam. "If it's a problem—"

Yes, it was a problem. If I had my way, she'd be naked. I cleared my throat. "No, it's fine." After an awkward pause, I tried to look at something other than her bare legs. "What are you doing?"

Her gaze crawled over my black boxer briefs, along my chest, and stopped at my lips for a long, heart-stopping moment. I probably should have put on pants. I'd been living alone so long, the thought had never occurred to me until then. Just another thing I had in common with Mr. H. The blatant heat in her eyes stirred my cock to life. I stepped behind the kitchen island to hide my arousal.

"It's an amazing invention called cooking," she said, rolling her eyes with a small smile. "I found a box of pancake mix and some bacon. I hope you don't mind."

"Mind? Hell, I'm ecstatic." I dragged a barstool from the island, my stomach rumbling enthusiastically, and took a seat across from her. On most mornings, I rolled out of bed, rumpled, smelling of stale beer and sex, to an empty apartment. If I was lucky, breakfast consisted of leftover pizza or takeout from the night before. Lately, I'd made the trek to Joe's Java Junction for espresso and one of Jo's specialty muffins. Having her in my kitchen was much, much better. She dropped a stack of pancakes onto a plate and nudged it toward me. My mouth watered at the sight of the golden circles of batter and her blue eyes. "I don't think anyone has ever cooked for me."

"Seriously?" With a hand on her hip, she searched my face. "Not even your mom?"

Sardonic laughter burned my throat. The idea of Honey in front of a stove tickled my funny bone. "The most my mother ever did was open a bag of potato chips and hand it to me. She was always too worried about her figure to eat and too obsessed with my father to care whether I ate or not."

The brightness of her eyes dimmed. I hated that look, one I'd seen so often in my childhood, tinged with pity. "What did you do?" She slid a bottle of warm syrup across the counter.

"I managed." I didn't want to dwell on the quiet nights, the empty house, or the loneliness that had characterized my childhood. The syrup drizzled over the golden pancakes, oozing over the sides with grand slowness. My mouth watered at the sight and scent of the gooey, sticky sweetness. "Most of the time I ate at Rhett's house. His mom loves me." I smirked to lighten the mood, but Jo remained somber, reminding me that a rift still existed between us, and I had no idea how to span the distance.

"Mealtime was fun around my house. Bronte and I would help my mom fix everything. She loved to cook and taught us all of the family recipes." She dipped a finger into the syrup on my plate and sucked it from her finger. I stared, mesmerized, remembering how her lips felt around my dick. I suppressed a groan and turned my attention to the food. The tip of her tongue swept over her lower lip. "I can't imagine what that was like for you."

"My family isn't normal." Since birth, I'd been trained to hide the relationship to my father, and to call my mother by her first name in public. She didn't like people to know she was old enough to have a twenty-nine-year-old son. As a result, I never spoke of my parents to anyone, not even Rhett.

"And mine is?" Her laughter rang across the table, warm and tinkling. The light returned to her eyes. "My dad spends his days and nights watching reality TV in his underwear. My sister is an autistic genius. I'm a stalker. No one would consider us normal."

I placed my fork beside the plate and lifted my eyes to meet hers. Unlike most of the people in my life, I knew I could trust her. She'd been forthright about the most embarrassing details of her past. I wanted to do the same, but I couldn't quite make the leap. "My mother is Honey Wilkes," I said, and waited for her to process this tidbit.

"Honey Wilkes." She rolled the name over her tongue, thinking. At last, her eyebrows lifted to her hairline. "*The* Honey Wilkes? From the music videos? No way."

"Yes way." Over the years, I'd become accustomed to people's reactions.

"She was very beautiful. No wonder you're so handsome," she said, a faint flush coloring her cheeks at the admission.

I shrugged. "She still is beautiful. She's the mistress of someone very famous and he got her pregnant, but he doesn't publicly claim me." It was the best I could do, the closest I'd ever come to admitting the truth about my birth.

"But you know who he is?" Soft, liquid eyes bored into mine.

"Yes, and he knows who I am. All this is the price of my silence." I waved a hand to encompass the building. The words sounded far away, like they were spoken by someone else, my voice altered by the thickness in my throat. I wanted to tell her everything, to confess the sordid details of my birth, to bury my face in her silky hair, to be comforted, but I couldn't continue. If I lowered the barrier around the vault of secrecy, I might break. "I stay away from him, and he stays out of my life. It's better this way for both of us."

"That must have been tough for you." The smoothness of her palm covered the rough back of my hand. I stared at it, warring with shame over my upbringing and the lust that followed every time she touched me.

"Yeah, well..." The topic of conversation rattled my nerves. I didn't want to think about all the ways life had shortchanged me. It didn't matter. Not anymore. The turmoil of my childhood had taught me to invest in the future. Nothing could be gained from lingering in the past. I moved my hand from beneath hers and shoved the pancakes away, my appetite destroyed.

"You don't like them? I usually make them from scratch. I did the best I could." The wounded expression in her eyes brought me up short, and I thought about someone else's feelings for a change.

"No. They're excellent." I cut a bite from the stack, dipped it in syrup, and held it up to her mouth. Her lips parted before enclosing around the fork. Our gazes locked. I'd never fed a woman before. The eroticism of the simple act caused lightning to flash low in my belly.

A drop of syrup landed on the corner of her mouth. I swiped it away with my thumb then rubbed the pad over her lower lip, spreading the syrup. Her tongue darted out to lick away the sticky residue. No matter how hard I tried, I couldn't pry my gaze from her mouth, that voluptuous, fuckable mouth.

Silence blanketed the room.

She looked away, breaking the delicate connection between us. "Well, I suppose, I should get dressed." She stood and glanced around like her tail was on fire and she needed to escape. "I'll come back and clean up the mess when you're done."

I watched her swinging backside move toward the door. I didn't want her to leave. "You don't have to clean up. The housekeeper will be here today."

"No. It's fine. It'll give me something to do." These last words were spoken over her shoulder, as if she didn't trust herself to look at me directly.

"Calloway—the attorney—he'll be here at ten," I called after her, remembering the grim task ahead of us.

She paused, extending a delicate hand to the door frame, but didn't turn around. "Okay." Then she disappeared into the darkened hallway, leaving me alone.

I don't know why it bothered me to see her leave. I should have been relieved. This was how I liked my life. Solitary. No responsibilities beyond work, getting laid, and keeping my ass out of trouble. I was always alone, always had been and always would be. Unless...I sat up straighter. The future was mine to choose.

Jo and I stood on a precipice with lies and misconceptions holding us apart. Before now, I'd never realized the fragility of our relationship. One wrong move could destroy any chance at calling her my girlfriend, because that was what I wanted, wasn't it? To make her mine? To care for her and about her? This feeling, the insatiable yearning, was uncharted territory. I had no idea how to begin a serious relationship. I'd almost ruined things by withholding knowledge of the warrant, by screwing her at the hotel before telling her, and by putting my selfish, animalistic needs in front of hers.

I huffed a heavy sigh and rubbed my forehead, hoping to clear the clutter of thoughts. Throughout my life, I'd always been a gambler, taking chances, risking everything to get what I wanted, everything but my heart. It was easy to risk it all when you had nothing to lose, but with Jo, the stakes were too high. If she rejected me again, I'd be crushed. The idea of failure tasted bitter, but the concept of doing nothing, of not trying, carried a higher penalty. How could I face myself in the mirror knowing I'd passed up the chance at something special without even trying?

CHAPTER 19

JO

Alan Calloway was a large man with a booming Texas drawl and hands the size of dinner plates. He dwarfed the suede club chair across from the sofa where I sat next to Carter. For more than two hours, he reviewed every detail of the charges filed against me, the night of the incident, and the circumstances of my breakup with Harold. I tried to focus on what he was saying, but it was difficult with Carter's muscular thigh pressing against mine, the heat of his body burning through my jeans, lighting my skin on fire.

"Lay it on us, Cal," Carter said. At first glance, he seemed relaxed, one arm thrown over the back of the couch behind me, his long legs stretched in front of him, but I could feel the tension inside him, coiled like a spring, lurking just beneath the surface of his calm.

"It's a good-news bad-news kind of thing," Calloway said, pushing his thick glasses up his nose with a forefinger. "Which do you want first?"

"Good news, please," I said. I clasped my hands in my lap, aware of the perspiration on my palms, hoping my nervousness didn't show.

"Fair enough." Calloway opened a folder on the coffee table and squinted at the contents. "The good news is that I had breakfast with the district attorney. Great little place over on Elm Street, has the best Scotch eggs in the world. Ever been there?" I shook my head. "The chef is from Edinburgh, and he came over here a few years ago to marry a girl from Laurel Falls." Carter scowled, and Calloway cleared his throat. "Well, anyway, given your lack of criminal record, the mitigating circumstances, and the D.A.'s personal dislike for your ex-fiancé, he's willing to cut a deal. The courts are overflowing right now. The jails are full. They're actually transferring inmates to other counties." He huffed. "The state of this county's government is in shambles. And with the recent uptick in drug use, they can't keep up with the—"

Carter interrupted, eyebrows lifting. "Cal, as I recall, I'm paying you an ungodly hourly rate. Do you think you could cut to the chase?"

"Right." He shuffled a few papers and blew out a breath, as if he'd lost his train of thought. "Anyway, you didn't actually steal anything, and you had a key to the property. The defendant failed to properly evict you from the premises, and your name is still on the lease, which means you retain a right to access the property. The prosecution will have a difficult time proving guilt without any evidence. If you plead guilty to the misdemeanor charge of trespass-ing, the felony charges of breaking and entering will be dropped. The bad news is that you'll have to pay a fine and be on probation for a short while, but that's a helluva lot better than jail time, don't you think?"

"Yes." Until this second, I hadn't realized I'd been holding my breath. I exhaled and rubbed my palms over my thighs. "Much better."

"What are her other options?" Carter asked.

"If you pass up the plea deal, it'll go to trial before a jury. You're looking at the possibility of a few years behind bars, although, like I said, they don't have much evidence, and the odds are in your favor. With the current backlog of cases, it won't go to trial for at least another three months. And you face the possibility of word getting out, something I'm sure you'll wish to avoid, given the reputation of your coffee shop."

"What about my dog?" I asked.

"I'm afraid there isn't much to be done there. You can sue for ownership in civil court. At the very least, you should file a counter-suit to regain your personal property and the cost of legal fees incurred by this frivolous indictment." He patted my hand, his smile sympathetic. "Goodness, you're white as a ghost."

"What do you think?" I asked, glancing at Carter uncertainly. He sat still as stone, chiseled features unreadable.

"Take the plea. This will all be over in a week, and you can move on with your life." He removed his spectacles, revealing kind hazel eyes. "Otherwise, you'll stand to lose a fortune in legal fees and time."

"Then that's what I'll do. I just want this to be over so I can move on with my life." Unable to withhold the sudden flood of relief and gratitude, I burst into tears. The gazes of Carter and Calloway bounced from me to each other and back again with a comical air of male helplessness and confusion. I raised a hand, laughing through the haze of tears. "It's okay. I'm fine. I'm just so—so relieved. You have no idea how much better I feel."

"Okay." Calloway's shoulders lowered. "Great."

"Thanks for taking this on with such short notice." Carter sprang into action, like he was eager to escape my overflowing emotions. "Let me walk you to the door, Cal."

Their deep masculine voices rumbled as they left the room. I buried my face in my hands and tried to get a grip on my vacillating feelings. While part of me mourned for Zipper, the other part rejoiced to know I wasn't going to jail. Now, I could put away the awkwardness between me and Carter. An unfamiliar melancholy threatened my newfound joy. I could go home now. Carter could go back to living his bachelor life. I took the elevator to the master suite and began throwing my things into my bag.

"What are you doing?" Carter loomed in the doorway as I closed the zipper.

"Packing." My heart galloped in my chest, partly from his presence and partly from the prospect of beginning my life anew. "Should I call a cab, or do you think I can catch one on the street?"

"Hold on. You're not going anywhere. Not yet." He stalked toward me, brows lowered. The breath caught in my throat at the sight of his penetrating brown eyes locked on mine.

"I'm not?"

"No." With gentle fingers, he pried the bag from my grip and set it on the floor. I sank onto the edge of the bed, feeling like my knees might give out if I stood for one second longer. "It's Friday. Calloway won't be able to meet with the D.A. until Monday. You need to stay low until he's had a chance to file the paperwork and have the arrest warrant withdrawn."

"Oh. Right." I stared at my toes on the jute rug, fighting the disappointment, until the tips of Carter's boots rested next to them.

He squatted in front of me, resting his forearms on the tops of his thighs so he was eye level with me. With a finger, he tilted up my chin. Our eyes met, and a tumultuous blend of lust and heat swirled through my chest. "Cheer up. It's not that bad, is it?"

"I'm just eager to get back to work, and I'm sure you're ready to have this place to yourself again."

The pad of his thumb caressed the point of my chin. Delicious desire shimmered beneath my skin. The spicy scent of his cologne wafted through the air. I wanted to throw myself on him, pull him down to the floor, and impale myself on the steel rod visible behind the fly of his jeans.

"You're welcome to stay here." If he was happy or disappointed to see me go, neither showed on his handsome face. Instead, he stood and looked down at me. "I've got to get back to the office. Think of this as a vacation. Relax. Hang out. Watch some TV. There's a library on the third floor. Read a book."

I watched him leave, feeling more confused than ever.

CHAPTER 20
CARTER

A few hours later, I sat in Rhett's office. He poured over a stack of reports while I stared into space. Outside the one-way glass wall, employees bustled about in conservative three-piece suits and dresses. Watching them renewed my happiness of being self-employed and free to wear anything I wanted. Although I admired Rhett's ambition and success, I could never spend my days chained to a corporate desk.

"I can hear your gears grinding," he said without looking up from his paperwork. "What kind of mayhem are you plotting today?"

"If you wanted to make an impression on a girl, how would you do it?" I blurted the question in my usual blunt, no-nonsense fashion. Rhett stared at me like I'd sprouted horns. A cold sweat sprung up on my chest. "Don't look at me like that."

His brows lowered in mock concern. "You're asking me for dating advice?" He dropped the papers, cocked his head, and picked up a pen.

"Don't be a dick." With an index finger, I circled the rim of my coffee cup, once, twice, then once again. "You're the only person I can ask shit like this."

"Anyone else would make you turn in your man card." He smirked, and I let him get away with it. Since grade school, I'd harassed him for his romantic notions, the way he'd wooed girls with his bright smile and sensitivity. While I'd been fucking the cheerleader captain beneath the bleachers, he'd been writing poems for the class valedictorian and winning the girls.

"Who, exactly, are you wanting to woo?" While he talked, he scribbled comments on a notepad.

"Don't say that."

"Say what?"

"'Woo.' It's weird and creepy."

"Alright. Who do you want to seduce?"

"Not that it's your business, but it's Jo."

His ink pen stopped moving mid-sentence. Very slowly, he lowered the pen, placing it alongside the computer keyboard. "Hold on a second." This was an obstacle I'd conveniently forgotten, his disapproval. He clasped his hands together and rested them on the desk between us. "Let me get this straight. You want a relationship? With Jo?"

"Sure. Who else? Keep up, Easton." I eased back in the chair, hiding my sudden anxiety beneath the cover of cockiness.

"I don't know. There have been so many others." The iron edge to his voice made me wince. "If you're just doing this so you can fuck her over later, I'll kick your ass."

Of course, he'd have reservations about my sincerity. "I'm serious." I scratched my beard. "I haven't been with anyone since Jo and I started fooling around, and I don't want anyone else."

"You say that today, but what happens two weeks or two months from now when things start to get tough? Or when you're out drinking with your buddies and a hot girl hits on you? She's like Bronte. The Hollander girls give one hundred percent to the people they love. Jo deserves someone who will love her back that way. Is that something you can do? Because, honestly, I'm not so sure."

Silence blanketed the room. I had no idea how to respond. Rhett, knowing me better than anyone, had touched upon all my weaknesses. I left my chair and went to the window. On the street below, people went about their daily lives. An elderly couple held hands as they walked along the tree-lined sidewalks. Unless I changed my ways, that would never be me. I'd been perfectly happy living a life of debauchery until my path had crossed with Jo. Now, the only future I wanted had her in it.

"I know I'm not good enough for her." During my life, people had constantly reminded me that I was an embarrassment or a nuisance or unworthy. "And I know my past is sketchy, to say the least, but if I don't try, I'll never forgive myself." When he didn't reply, I turned around to find him grinning at me like a psychopath. I glowered at him. "You think this is funny?"

"Hell yes. I've been waiting for this moment for years." He shifted in his chair, still smiling. "Just give me a minute. I want to enjoy this." His shoulders began to shake with laughter.

"Thanks a lot. I'm glad you find my heartbreak amusing. You've been a great help." My menacing glare did nothing to assuage his amusement.

He dabbed at the moisture in his eyes. "No, seriously. Since we were kids, I've been dreaming about the day you fell in love. Just once. And now you've gone and fallen for the one person least likely to return your feelings." I raised my middle finger, causing his smile to widen. "Yes, this is an amazing day. What next?"

"Maybe monkeys will fly out of your butt. That would make me feel a whole lot better."

"Alright." He lifted a hand, his expression sobering. "I'm sorry. Wait, no I'm not." The smile returned. "But if you're truly sincere, I'm willing to help."

CHAPTER 21

JO

After Carter left, I curled up on the chenille loveseat in the library with an enticing book. I hadn't read anything more than ingredient labels and recipes in over a year and relished the thought of losing myself in a good novel. With a cozy afghan for snuggling, I tucked a foot underneath me and tried to concentrate on the prose. Everything smelled like Carter, and my thoughts kept going back to the way he'd taken me at the hotel. He'd been gentle but relentless. I'd never been fucked so thoroughly in my life. I touched a hand to my lips, remembering his brutal kisses. He'd physically used me, and I'd loved every minute of it.

Just thinking of his narrow hips pumping between my legs sent a rush of heat into my cheeks and dampness into my panties. No one had ever made me come so hard or so many times. His rough hands had been tender and commanding. "No," I whispered at the lurch of my heart. I had to keep a clear head. This confusing rush of endorphins and hormones wasn't love. It was lust, pure and simple. I couldn't allow sexual attraction to develop into feelings. To fall in love with Carter would be committing emotional suicide. Even if he recanted his denial and wanted to start a relationship, I'd be crazy to accept. Or would I? The challenge of taming him tantalized and tempted me. If he asked again, would I accept? How could I not?

"Hello?" A female voice floated up from the ground floor. "Is anyone home?" Light footsteps traveled along the hardwood floor, followed by the clanging metal and grinding gears of the elevator.

"Shit." My pulse tripled. Carter hadn't said he was expecting company. The housekeeper had come and gone. I bit my lower lip and tried to prepare for the worst, an ex-girlfriend or a lover.

"Oh, hi." A tall, platinum blonde stood in the hallway, arms filled with garment bags and packages. "You must be Jo." Her gaze raked over my body, assessing, stopping short of my face.

"Um, hi." Embarrassment heated my cheeks. "I'm sorry. I don't know who you are."

"Darcy." Still avoiding eye contact, she dropped the items on the desk. "Carter asked me to pick up a few things for you to wear for the wedding." I cast a skeptical eye over her purple flowered shirt and red leggings. She caught my glance and rolled her eyes. "Relax. My sister is a personal shopper at Neiman Marcus."

"Thanks," I said, choosing brevity of speech as the safest of my choices until I figured her out.

"I've got several options here for you. Try them on. I'll return whatever you don't like or doesn't fit. I got two different sizes of each outfit. There are two long gowns and two cocktail dresses, matching lingerie, and shoes."

"I appreciate your help," I said, hoping to convey my heartfelt sincerity. "I'm sure it's not your job to find clothing for Carter's dates." At least, I hoped it wasn't.

She scoffed. "You wouldn't believe the things he asks me to do. And always texting me in the middle of the night. I swear that guy never sleeps." With a hand on each hip, she shook her head, long earrings swinging like pendulums.

I fingered the edge of a navy silk dress. "Have you worked for him a long time?"

"A few years." The weight of her stare dragged over me once

more, and I got the feeling that I came up lacking in her analysis. "Long enough to know his likes and dislikes. Long enough to see a hundred girls like you come and go."

Wow. The back of my neck prickled. "What's that supposed to mean?" I caught her gaze. Disapproval and protectiveness clouded her eyes, more like a mother hen than a girlfriend. A bit of the tension in my shoulders eased. Her attitude stemmed from affection, not cattiness.

"It means that Carter doesn't do relationships. So if you think you're going to take advantage of his good heart or his fat bank account, you've got another thing coming."

I drew in a short, sharp breath, offended by her statement. "My relationship with Carter isn't any of your business." The depth of my resentment caught me by surprise.

"Well, that's where you're wrong. He *is* my business." Darcy's mouth pinched into a tight line.

I drew a shaking hand across my forehead. The conversation had gone from unpleasant to uncomfortable in less than a minute. Most people liked me without any effort on my part. Judging by the scowl on her neon-pink lips, it would take a lot more than smiles and pleasantries to win her over. "You care a lot for him."

Her expression softened, but her eyes remained steely. "Carter's a good man, the best boss I've ever had, and it's my job to watch out for him. God knows his mother won't do it, and his father doesn't give a shit about him. He needs someone to have his back."

The level of concern in her voice eased my animosity. I could never fault a person for defending another, especially when I'd done the same so many times in my life. "He's very lucky to have you."

"No. I'm the lucky one. When we met, I had three kids, no job, no home, and we were starving. Carter made me his assistant, found us a house, and made sure we had enough to eat until I got back on my feet." Her face glowed as she spoke, making my heart squeeze. "Most people think he's an ass, but I know the truth. He's generous to a fault, and underneath his hard exterior, he's easily hurt."

"You don't have to worry. I'm not going to hurt him." In fact, I had a feeling it was my own heart on the line. I'd sworn off men, but Carter had managed to sneak past every barrier I'd erected.

We stared at each other. I lifted my chin, matching her stubborn will with my own. Faced with Darcy's absolute disapproval, I found my resolve to push Carter away weakening.

"Never say never," she remarked, her tone airy. "I'm sure I don't need to point out that you owe him a lot, too. He's gone above and beyond to get you out of this crazy mess you're in. Kept me awake half the night digging up dirt on your ex, calling in favors from the D.A. I hope you're worth the trouble."

"I know. You're right." I'd been so consumed by my personal challenges that I'd trivialized Carter's efforts. If it wasn't for him, I'd be sitting in a jail cell right now, facing a handful of felony charges and a prison sentence. I sank into the nearest chair and dropped my head into my hands. "How can I ever repay him?"

A gentle hand patted my shoulder. "You seem like a nice girl—crazy, but nice." I looked up into Darcy's worried eyes. "Be nice to him. He's used to being ignored and overlooked, so he fights against any kindness, but once you've won him over, he'll never let you down."

"You really care about him," I said, surprised by the emotion in my voice. "I care about him, too."

"Then don't play with his heart," she said, turned around, and left.

CHAPTER 22

CARTER

When I left Jo earlier that day, she'd been curled up on the loveseat in the library, reading a romance novel. When I returned home, I found her in the same place. I stood in front of her for several minutes before she noticed me, enjoying the soft curve of her parted lips, the faint glimmer of tears in her eyes. Finally, she lowered the book and stretched lazily, like a cat, a smile bowing her mouth.

That strange, unexplained twist happened again, the one that tightened my balls and seized my heart. I smiled back at her. The presence of a female in the sanctity of my library turned the world upside down. Never before had something so wrong seemed so right.

"You're home already? I can't believe it's so late. I totally lost track of time." She closed the book and placed it on the small table at her side. She glanced up and her eyes went wide. "Oh, my gosh. You cut your hair, and your beard—it's gone."

"Yeah, what do you think?" I rubbed a hand over the smoothness of my jaw, unused to the feel of bare skin. After my visit with Rhett, taking Reagan's threats to heart, I'd gone to the nearest barber and gotten a complete overhaul. The lion's mane was gone, less than an inch long on the sides, long enough on the top to be edgy and anti-establishment.

"You look different. Amazing. Dangerous." A slow smile lifted one corner of her mouth. "I like it."

"Thanks." Embarrassed by her praise, I grinned sheepishly and took a seat beside her, ignoring the dryness of my mouth and the trembling of my hands. I'd never been this nervous around a woman before, mostly because I'd never cared what any woman thought of me. To change the subject away from myself, I asked, "What are you reading?"

"*Raintree County*," she said. "Have you read it?"

"Yeah. It's good." We stared at each other for a beat. My hands rested on the tops of my thighs, fingers curled against the urge to sweep the hair from her face. "Have you been up here all day?"

"Pretty much." A dimple appeared in her left cheek, one I'd never noticed before.

"Did you have anything to eat?"

"No, I was too engrossed in the book, but I am a little hungry." She stretched again, groaning, the sound agitating my libido.

"Great. I've got pizza downstairs. I thought we could eat and maybe watch a movie or something." I stood and offered my hand to help her up. She rolled her lips together, thinking, then slid her palm over mine. Our fingers curled together as I pulled her to her feet.

After pizza, Jo chose an action thriller movie and fell asleep halfway through, curled up on the sofa, her head pillowed in my lap. I stared at her, the lacy fan of eyelashes on her cheeks, her parted lips, and the slow rise and fall of her breasts with each breath. She looked so innocent and vulnerable. I wanted to scoop her into my arms and protect her from all the evil in the world. When the movie ended, I clicked off the television and wondered what I should do next. I'd sat next to her for the past two hours, an uncomfortable erection in my pants and a knot in the pit of my stomach. This new and uncharted territory had me on edge. The old Carter would have dragged her to the floor and stripped away her clothes before the opening credits of the movie. The new Carter had waited patiently throughout the entire film, casting covert glances at her, worrying if she was too hot or too cold, thirsty or uncomfortable. I rubbed a hand over my bare neck, where my long hair had once been.

"I should probably go to bed." Jo sat up and blinked sleepy eyes at me, covering a yawn. "What time are we leaving for the wedding tomorrow?"

"It's an hour drive to the church, so I guess we should leave by two. That'll give us plenty of time."

"Do you think it's okay for me to go out like that? I mean, you're not worried someone will recognize me?" She tucked her hair behind her ear and pulled her bottom lip between her teeth.

"You're not connected to any of the guests, it's out of town, and Calloway will be there." I rubbed perspiring palms over my jeans. There were things about myself that she should know before meeting my father, important things, but fear and shame kept the secrets locked inside me. "About the wedding—" The end of the sentence disappeared from my head. My heart began to palpitate so badly I thought my chest would explode.

"What is it?" The weight of her gaze on my face tripled my anxiety.

Jesus, Carter. Talk. I cleared my throat and tried again. "I hope it's not too boring." *What a coward.*

"Aren't they all?" The long waves of her hair shimmered as she shook her head. "Don't worry. I'll be on my best behavior. It's the least I can do after everything you've done for me." I sat there staring at her like an idiot. She bent and placed a kiss on my cheek, stopping my heart in its tracks.

Tell her. Tell her you love her. Tell her you made a mistake, that you can do relationships, that you want a chance with her. Tell. Her.

The words traveled through my head on a loop, but the only thing that came out of my mouth was, "No problem."

We went upstairs together, parting at our respective rooms.

All night long, I tossed and turned, thinking of her on the other side of the bedroom wall, sleeping in my bed, on my sheets. I should be there with her, holding her against my chest, keeping her warm and protected in my arms. In all of my life experiences, I'd never been a coward, not in front of enemy soldiers, nor when chasing down a fugitive. Tomorrow, after the wedding, I'd tell her I loved her, because the risk of letting her go seemed so much worse.

CHAPTER 23

JO

The wedding was held at an enormous cathedral known for its celebrity connections. We sat at the back, on the bride's side. I wiped nervous palms along the skirt of my gown and tried not to gape at the familiar faces of congressmen, senators, judges, and dignitaries. Calloway sat a few rows in front of us and nodded in welcome when we took our seats.

Carter shifted restlessly in the pew. The classic lines of his tuxedo emphasized his broad shoulders and narrow waist. The contrast of sophistication with his raw, primal energy made my blood sing. One of his arms rested along the backrest behind me, his fingers toying with the strap of my gown. His black-clad legs crammed beneath the pew in front of us, knees spread wide, brushing my thigh. I fanned my face with the program to dispel some of the internal heat blasting inside me.

Everyone stood for the entrance of the bride, but most eyes focused on Carter. Their stares went beyond the boundaries of polite interest. He remained immobile, chin lifted, expression implacable. Once we resumed our seats, I rested a hand on his thigh. The muscle tensed under my palm. After a few seconds, he smiled down at me and engulfed my hand in his larger one.

He leaned down to whisper in my ear. "I hate these things." Our eyes met, and my core clenched. With an index finger, he brushed a strand of hair away from my face. "Thanks again for coming with me."

"You're welcome." The praise filled me with warmth. "I'm never getting married, but if I do, it won't be like this," I replied, gazing over the endless guests, the eight bridesmaids, and the stifling air of cere-mony. I ran a hand over his shaven cheek where stubble had already begun to sprout. He was the kind of guy who needed to shave multiple times a day. He smiled beneath my touch.

"Careful," he said, his eyes darkening. "I'm thinking some very sinful thoughts about you right now. I don't want to get struck by lightning."

"Shhhh," someone admonished, sending me into a fit of muted giggles. Disproving faces turned to glare at us. Carter stared back at them. I bit my lower lip and glanced down, my gaze falling on our clasped hands. His thumb smoothed over the back of my hand, causing me to have a few illicit thoughts of my own.

Two hours later, we drove across the city to the reception. As we entered the enormous ballroom of the Elysian Palace Hotel, nervous butterflies tumbled in my belly. I knew at a glance that I was in way over my head. At my side, Carter simmered with unrest. Anxiety emanated from every line of his body. He hadn't spoken a word throughout the wedding or during the drive to the reception. I glanced over at him, hoping to discern his mood, but he'd drawn the familiar shutter over his eyes.

The crystal chandeliers reflected off the polished floors as we crossed the room. Hundreds of guests gathered around white-and-silver tables. The family and wedding party surrounded a long table at the front. We were seated at a small table by ourselves, all the way in the rear next to the kitchen. No one spoke to us. Carter remained tight-lipped and strained during the meal, his unrest growing with each passing course. Afterward, I excused myself to freshen up, thinking I'd done something to offend him. I took a wrong turn and bumbled into a small reception room. Before I could leave, the doors opened and a couple entered.

"What is he doing here?" the woman asked. Venom laced her voice. I recognized her as the mother of the bride.

"I have no idea." The man, whom I recognized as Senator Mayfield, paused to straighten the knot of his bowtie in a nearby mirror. "Don't worry about it."

"Of course I'm worried. He's an embarrassment." She paced the floor in front of the doors, her high heels clicking on the tile. "It's one thing for you to have a mistress. It's another thing to flaunt your bastard son under my nose."

"Calm down." He smoothed a hand over his hair then straightened his cuffs. "No one knows or cares that Carter is here."

His dismissive tone stabbed me in the gut. My heart squeezed for Carter. No wonder he'd been so silent. This explained the stares, the whispers, and the general dismissal of his presence. He was the Senator's son. I'd never voted for the man, turned off by rumors of dirty politics and dishonest tactics.

"It matters to me," she said. "You and I have an agreement. I play the happy homemaker, and you keep your sordid sex life away from our family. I want you to get rid of him. Now."

Senator Mayfield smiled at his reflection, pleased with what he saw. Arrogant ass. From my hiding place, I got a good view of his face. I bit my lower lip to hold back a gasp. How did I miss the resemblance? Father and son shared the same amber eyes, sun-streaked brown hair, and sharp features. Aside from Carter's greater height, the genetic connection between the two men was unmistakable.

"You make it sound like you're the poor wounded wife, when we both know you've been screwing the golf pro at the country club for months now." He tweaked the knot in his tie once more. "Don't worry about Carter. He's been paid well to keep his mouth shut."

I didn't hear the rest of the conversation. I stumbled through a back door. The remnants of my dinner rose to the back of my throat as the pieces of the puzzle fell into place. The bride was Carter's sister, and the senator was his father. After a quick stop at the powder room to regain my composure, I hastened back to the reception. I thought about all the covert glances and snide whispers and his proud stare. He needed me.

I found Carter standing alone on the terrace, staring pensively over the gardens. Torches danced over the profusion of blooms and blossoms. A full moon cast blue light into the shadows and sharpened his features. I slipped my hand into his, no longer caring about the petty boundaries of our relationship.

"Why didn't you tell me the senator was your dad?" I asked after a lengthy silence.

His chest lifted and fell with a deep breath. He continued to gaze out over the garden. "Because I signed an NDA when I received my trust fund. I can't publicly acknowledge who my father is."

I tightened my grip on his fingers. "Is that why no one has spoken to us?"

"Yes." His Adam's apple bobbed up and down. My admiration for him increased tenfold. He looked so proud, yet I knew he was hurting inside.

"So everyone knows?"

He shrugged. "If they don't know, I'm sure they suspect. I mean, look at us. It doesn't take a genius to figure it out."

Anger on his behalf swelled inside me. "You know what? Fuck those people. You don't need any of them. We don't have to stay. You don't have to put up with this shit."

"I agree." A male voice replied from behind us. We turned in unison to find the senator standing outside the doors, a champagne flute in one hand and a cigar in the other. "You should go."

The two men glared at each other. Carter lifted his chin. He tried to lose my hand, but I held fast. I refused to abandon him when he needed a friend. After a second, his grip tightened. When he spoke, his voice was tight and raw. "I'm not here for you. I came to support Reagan."

"Daddy, what's going on?" The bride floated onto the terrace. The lace layers of her designer gown ruffled in the light breeze. She was a vision of loveliness, if somewhat tipsy.

"I was just telling Carter that it's getting late, and he should probably be leaving." By his tone, the senator was used to giving orders and having them obeyed.

"Nonsense." She lifted her skirts and shouldered between father and son.

"I suppose you think this is funny, inviting him here," the senator said, a muscle ticking in his cheek.

"No. I'm thrilled to have him here, and you should be too." Rebellion glittered in her eyes. On tiptoe, she placed a kiss on Carter's cheek. He stood like stone, solid and unmoving. "Thank you for coming. It means a lot to me." As she descended, her gaze fell on me. She extended a gloved hand. "I don't believe we've met. I'm Reagan, and you must be Josephine Hollander."

"Just Jo," I said.

"And this is my father, Senator Mayfield," she said. Her use of *my* instead of *our* grated over my nerves. Then again, I supposed that she'd been groomed to avoid all reference to her relationship with Carter. They had tried to erase him from their lives. Having experienced the love of a wonderful father, my heart ached for him.

"It's a pleasure to meet you, Jo," he said, but he didn't offer his hand to shake, and neither did I. My dislike for him grew greater by the minute. What kind of man shunned his son, made him feel unwanted and unloved? I'd never hated anyone more than Harold, but Senator Mayfield was quickly becoming the top contender for the honor.

"I wish I could say the same," I replied, not caring if I was rude. Carter's eyebrows shot up, amusement bowing his mouth.

The four of us stood in awkward silence. Carter's eyes glowed with suppressed animosity. He was like a lion who'd been caged too long, his tail jerking with the need to pounce.

"Could you ladies excuse us for a minute?" the senator said, his eyes locking with Carter's.

"Are you going to be nice?" Reagan lifted her chin and bounced her gaze between them.

"I'm always nice," Carter and his father said in unison.

"I could use a drink," I said. A cold beer sounded heavenly, although I had a suspicion it would take more than alcohol to erase this night from my memory.

"You're welcome to stay, Jo." Carter lifted my hand and pressed his lips to the back. The anger and heat in his eyes made gooseflesh ripple along my arms.

"Has she signed an NDA?" the senator asked.

"She doesn't need one," Carter said. "Unlike you, I trust the people around me."

"That's why you're an idiot." The senator puffed on his cigar, sending frothy white clouds of smoke into a halo around his head.

"On second thought, Jo, why don't you check out the bar? I'll meet you there in a few minutes." Carter's gaze remained locked with this father's, animosity thickening the air.

"I should get back to my guests," Reagan said. She bit her lower lip and shifted from side to side. "Walk with me, Jo?"

"Sure." My fingers slipped through Carter's as we parted. I hated to leave him alone with this hateful man. "Would you like me to get something for you?"

"No, I'm fine." Our eyes met, and I saw that he was reassuring me about more than drinks.

"It's better to let them fight it out alone," Reagan said as we walked away. She cast a worried glance over her shoulder. "I hope they don't get out of hand."

"Does this happen often?"

"Every time they see each other. Daddy likes to push Carter's buttons. It's always been that way." She paused near a pair of French doors and placed a hand on my arm to halt my steps. "Do you mind if we stop for a minute? This dress weighs a million pounds, and I'm burning up." She opened the doors and stepped into the refreshing breeze. "I can't wait to get out of this thing."

"It's very beautiful." Exquisite cut glass beads twinkled in the lights. A gown like that probably cost more money than I made in a year.

"Thanks. It seems like a waste to spend so much money on something you only wear once. I'll probably donate it to charity or something." Her gloved hand smoothed over the bodice before her bright eyes turned to mine. "You don't have to worry about Carter. He can take care of himself."

I strained for sounds of their voices, but the rustle of wind through the trees and the orchestra in the ballroom muffled any sounds. Reagan continued to scrutinize my face. I turned my attention to the view.

"Have you known Carter very long?" she asked. I couldn't tell if she was making small talk or fishing for information.

"Not very. His best friend is dating my sister."

"But you guys are seeing each other? Like, dating?"

I bit my lower lip. I had no idea how to explain our relationship. Over the past few days, the intensity of our connection had escalated to something more than friendship, but neither of us had put a name to it. "We're friends. Good friends."

"I see." Kicking off her shoes, she sank into a chair with a groan. "That feels amazing." Her eyes closed, and her head tipped back. "He doesn't date, you know. I told him he had to bring someone, that he couldn't come alone, just to force him out of his comfort zone. At this rate, he's going to be single forever, and he deserves to be with someone nice and kind who loves him."

"Yes, he does." I appreciated her concern for a brother she couldn't claim. "It must be hard for him to watch your family—his family—and not be able to participate in it."

"I know, right?" She sat up abruptly, eyes flashing. "It's total bullshit. This is the twenty-first century. People have illegitimate kids all the time. Daddy could handle this if he wanted to. If I had my way, it wouldn't be a secret." Her shoulders slumped, and she leaned back again. "I threatened to tell everyone, but Daddy is a powerful man. He can be very persuasive when he wants. Better watch out. Next thing you know, he'll have you signing an NDA too."

I blinked at her admission. "He made you sign a non-disclosure agreement? His daughter?"

"Sure. All the kids had to sign one when they reached eighteen. Our family has too many secrets. There's nothing Daddy values more than his career and reputation." The edges of her words slurred the tiniest bit, although her actions remained crisp. I couldn't blame her for getting drunk at her own wedding. In fact, it sounded like a fantastic idea. "When Daddy insisted I marry this guy, I said no way. I mean, he's nice and everything, but he's a little bit intimidating, don't you think?" She waved a hand. "Anyway, he—Daddy—gave me a nice, fat dowry and the down payment on a house in the country, so I agreed. After all, if you can't be happy, you might as well be rich."

My mouth dropped open. From watching Dad's reality shows, I knew the wealthy lived a different type of existence from my middle-class lifestyle, but I had no idea arranged marriages existed in the present day and age. Apparently, the NDA didn't extend to the terms of her marriage.

"I can see by your expression that I've shocked you." Her giggle rang across the patio. "It's what we do—blackmail each other. Think of it as a chess game. You move. I counter."

"Would you like me to get you something from the bar?" I asked, eager to escape, glancing toward the open doors, and freedom.

"You know, Carter's a good person. He's not like us. I'm so jealous of him. I mean, he gets to live a normal life without all of this." She swept a hand to encompass the sea of colorful guests, the gleaming silver table service, the dozens of wait staff eager to fulfill her every wish. "I hope you appreciate him."

"He is. I do." I stumbled backward into a hard chest. I gazed up into the groom's dark, handsome face. He caught me by the elbows and held on until I steadied my footing.

"There you are," he said to Reagan. "Why are you hiding back here?"

"My feet hurt," she said with a small smile and a sigh of resignation. "Have you met Jo Hollander? Jo, this is my husband, Davis Jardine. Jo is Carter's date."

"Very nice to meet you," he said. I nodded. Something about him made me nervous, something I couldn't quite put a finger on. I could understand Reagan's hesitance to marry such a commanding person. In a stern voice, he commanded, "Jesus, Reagan, you're drunk as a skunk. Put your shoes on. We need to mingle. This will be over in a few hours, and you can get as shitfaced as you want then. In fact, I'll join you." He gave me a tight, apologetic nod. "Excuse us, Ms. Hollander. We must get back to the other guests."

"No problem," I replied. "And congratulations."

Davis gave Reagan's arm a short jerk. She scowled and yanked her arm away from him. "Straighten up," he growled.

"You're not the boss of me." With a tip of her chin, she collected her wits and strolled through the double doors. "Good evening, Jo. Take care of Carter for me."

"I will," I said, and followed them into the vast ballroom. They melted into the crowd amid hugs and exclamations. Reagan smiled and flitted from one person to the next while her husband kept a watchful eye on her. I made a mental note to ask Carter about their story later.

Snippets of conversation caught my ears as I wandered through the reception, talk of yachts and private jets and vacations in places I'd only seen on television. Each passing second reminded me that I didn't fit in here and never would. While these people brokered deals worth millions of dollars and debated the merits of caviar over pâté, I'd be slinging coffee and struggling to pay the bills. Their problems seemed trivial and ridiculous, and I had to wonder if any of them had ever faced true adversity.

Unable to stomach another second of curious glances and thinly veiled whispers, I veered toward the open bar. While I waited for the bartender to mix my drink, a slender girl in a blue-and-silver gown fell into line behind me, her silky hair in an elegant updo. She moved to my side on a subtle cloud of gardenia perfume, the silk and organza hem of her dress swirling gracefully around her feet.

"It's a lovely wedding, isn't it?" she asked.

I glanced over my shoulder before realizing she was talking to me. "Um, yes. It's beautiful."

"I'm engaged and planning our wedding. Nothing as extravagant as this, but I've gotten some wonderful ideas." Although we'd never met, something about her seemed familiar. I tried not to stare while taking in her profile. Maybe she was a celebrity of some sort, or a politician's wife.

"Congratulations," I said.

We both reached for a cocktail napkin at the same time, our fingers brushing.

She laughed and withdrew her hand. "Oh, excuse me. I'm so sorry. Harold always says I have bad timing."

Recognition dawned like the scratch of nails on a chalkboard. I tilted my head and looked up into her face. This was the girl—the floozy—my replacement. No wonder he'd chosen her over me. She was tall and lovely and cultured, everything I wasn't.

"Are you a friend of the bride or the groom?" she asked.

"Neither." The tip of my tongue stuck to the roof of my dry mouth. I swallowed, licked my lips, and tried again. "I mean, my date is a friend of the bride." The bartender handed my drink to me. Someone jostled me from behind. Liquor splashed over the rim of the glass and dribbled down the front of my dress. "Crap." I glanced around, searching for a place to set my glass and a napkin to dab the spill.

"Oh no. That's going to leave a terrible stain. Do you have any club soda and a clean towel?" she asked the bartender. Once he'd passed the items to her, she began dabbing at the dark patches on the fabric, forcing me to stay in her presence a few moments longer. "This will take it right out. Such a shame too. Your dress is beautiful. Where did you get it?"

"I'm not sure where it came from. It was a gift from my date," I said between gritted teeth. Not only did she know how to remove stains; she was nice, too. I wanted to hate her, but it was impossible.

"He sounds like a wonderful guy. My Harold couldn't even begin to pick out a dress half this nice. He has no sense of fashion."

"I hope he doesn't break your heart," I murmured, suddenly feeling sympathy for her.

"Pardon me?" She smiled at me, her face hopeful and earnest and filled with positivity.

"Nothing." I returned her smile. It wasn't her fault that Harold was a douche. "Thank you for the help."

"No problem." She dabbed a few more times at the bodice of my gown then shrugged. "Once it dries, it should be good as new—well, almost. Be sure to get it to the cleaner's first thing tomorrow."

"I will." I set the champagne flute on the tray of a passing waiter and scanned the room for Carter's tousled hair and broad shoulders. What was taking so long? Panic nudged my composure. I didn't want to risk running into Harold. I needed to leave and soon.

"There's my fiancé." She waved to someone behind me, and my stomach dropped to the floor. The sea of strangers pressed in from all sides. From three tables away, a familiar pair of eyes met mine, eyes I never thought to see again, and definitely not at a stranger's wedding.

CHAPTER 24

JO

Harold's mouth dropped open. I blinked in shock. The air vacated the room, leaving me in a vacuum. To my credit, I managed to maintain my composure better than he did. Although a dozen yards separated us, his shock reverberated across the distance. After a prolonged period of awkward staring, he sprang into action, excusing himself from his conversation and striding toward me.

I glanced around the ballroom, searching for the nearest exit or an alcove to disappear into. People hemmed me in on all sides. I maneuvered between a congressman and his wife, muttering apologies, but it was too late. Harold stepped in front of me, displeasure creasing his forehead.

"Jo? I thought that was you. What are you doing here?" At the sound of his voice, an unpleasant emptiness filled my stomach. This was the way it had always felt to be with him, like I'd done something wrong, like I fell short in every manner.

"I was invited," I replied, unable to eliminate the defensiveness in my tone.

"She's my date," Carter said from somewhere close behind me. I exhaled the breath I'd been holding. The warmth of his palm rested on the small of my back, strong and reassuring. "I don't think we've been introduced. I'm Carter Eckhouse."

"Harold Rodgers." Although he extended a hand to Carter, his gaze roved over me, still disbelieving. "I hardly recognized you. You look so different."

"Really? You look exactly the same." I fought to keep my tone steady, even though my knees trembled. Next to Carter's powerful frame, Harold seemed frail and feminine. "I didn't realize you knew the Mayfields."

"I don't. My fiancée is a cousin of the groom." I winced at his reference to the woman who'd replaced me. She stared at us, her smile drifting into a frown of confusion. By dumping me, he'd advanced his position in society. "Shouldn't you be in jail?" he asked, his eyes hardening. "You missed your court date."

"I—um—" I floundered in the effort to make a snappy comeback. Why did he make me feel so inadequate? Frustration and anger welled up inside me.

"Harold?" His fiancée placed a hand on his forearm. Her eyes widened in warning. "Don't make a scene."

"This is Jo. I've told you about her. She's the one who broke into my apartment."

"*Our* apartment," I said, finding my voice at last. "You know, the one with my name on the lease."

"Any questions for Ms. Hollander will need to be directed to me. She's retained my services as legal counsel," Calloway said, stepping from behind Carter.

Harold smiled, his gaze bouncing from me to Calloway and back again. "Is this a joke?"

"Ms. Hollander has filed a countersuit for compensation owed to her in the loss of her apartment and possessions as well as damages resulting from her wrongful arrest. I've also submitted a request to drop the protective order." He gave me a shrewd smile. "In the meantime, I'd suggest you lawyer up, Mr. Rodgers, because we'll be suing the proverbial pants off you."

The color drained from Harold's already pale face. "Jo, you can't be serious."

I opened my mouth to speak, but Calloway lifted a finger to stop me. "Ms. Hollander has nothing further to say, Mr. Rodgers. If you have any requests, you can have your attorney contact me on Monday. Now, I suggest you go back to your side of the room and leave my client in peace."

I watched Harold slink away, his confused fiancée trotting on his heels. "You couldn't possibly have done all that on a weekend," I said to Calloway.

He gave me a wink. "No, but he doesn't know that."

"That guy's a dick," Carter said, looking down at me.

"I realize that," I replied dryly. Had I been so desperate for a boyfriend that I'd overlooked Harold's obvious flaws? Nothing about his personality or appearance appealed to me anymore. All I could think about was how imposing Carter looked standing next to him, how I wanted to run my fingers through his hair and rain kisses on his handsome face.

"I'll see you in my office next week Ms. Hollander," Calloway said. "If you'll excuse me, my wife is giving me a dirty look. Apparently, I'm in trouble again." He winked and downed his bourbon in one gulp. "You two have a lovely evening."

"Thanks, I appreciate your help."

He extended a hand. I took it in both of mine and gave him a smile. With a parting nod, he weaved his way across the room and disappeared into the crowd.

Carter's hand moved lower on my back to the upper swell of my buttock and squeezed. Warmth returned to his eyes as he gazed down at me. "Shall we get the fuck out of here?"

"I thought you'd never ask," I said, breathing a sigh of relief.

He yanked on the tail of his bowtie, pulled it from his collar, and dropped it onto the tray of a passing waiter. The rough grasp of his hand found mine, threading through my fingers. "What's the quickest way to the parking lot?" he asked the waiter.

"Through the French doors to the terrace. Down the path on the left." He pointed a finger toward the gardens. "Around the bend and past the gazebo."

"Thanks." He gave the man a nod and pulled me in the indicated direction.

I trotted next to him, heels tapping on the ballroom floor. We breezed past the other guests and onto the terrace. Carter unbuttoned the collar of his shirt. Our feet crunched on the gravel, my heels tottering on the uneven surface. He gripped my hand tighter.

"Slow down. I'm going to break an ankle." I winced as the stones cut through the thin soles of my shoes. "Wait. Just a second." I kicked off my shoes and picked them up by the straps, letting them dangle from the fingers of my free hand.

"Better?"

"Yes." Something about the way he looked at me erased the bitter taste left by the encounter with Harold.

"Come on," he said, in his gruff voice.

Clasping hands again, we ran across the lawn toward the parking lot and freedom. The cool grass tickled my bare feet. The sprinklers erupted before we reached the other side. Droplets of water arched through the air. He tugged me through the spray, his eyes dark and playful. His mischievous nature was one of the things I loved best about him, and he never failed to surprise me. If he'd been affected by the words of his father, he didn't act like it.

"You're ruining my dress," I said.

"I'll buy you another one." The promise in his tone made my pulse leap. Did that mean we weren't over yet? I'd assumed the end of the weekend would signal the end of our relationship. I wished, with all my heart, that I was wrong.

CHAPTER 25

CARTER

The drive home flashed past in a blur of laughter and smiles. I hadn't felt this lighthearted since—well, ever. This had been one of the best and worst weeks of my life. I'd faced down the judgmental stares of my father's crowd and lived to tell about it. Having Jo at my side, seeing her with Harold, hearing his condescending words, made me realize how inconsequential my problems were. Those people—Reagan and Senator Mayfield—they might be my blood relations, but they weren't my family. I could pick and choose how much influence they carried in my life.

Behind Jo's smiles, I sensed the wheels turning in her brain. Was she obsessing over Harold? I wanted to ask but couldn't bear to hear the answer if she said yes. All I could think about was how badly I wanted her, how much I wanted this euphoria to continue beyond tonight and tomorrow and the next day and the next.

When we reached home, she went straight to the elevator. "I can't wait to get out of this dress," she said. "Can you undo my zipper?" With her right hand, she swept her hair to one side, baring the slim column of her neck.

"Sure." My hand trembled as I pulled on the tab. I blamed it on the vibration of the elevator and the aged mechanism. The dress gave way, slipping down to her shoulders. She caught it to her chest with one hand. I longed to run a finger down the groove of her spine and press a kiss to the soft skin between her shoulder blades, because I was gone—totally, completely, and irretrievably gone—for her.

"Are you hungry? Because I'm starved," she said. "I could go for some leftover pizza."

"Sounds good. I'll bring some up."

After changing into a pair of sweats, I brought up the pizza and a couple of cold beers. I entered my bedroom, pulse sprinting. Jo came out of the bathroom, rubbing her cotton candy lotion onto her hands, the sweet scent setting fire to my blood, wearing my T-shirt again, her hair spilling down her back. There was something oddly normal about the scene, like she belonged here, like we did this every day. And how great would that be? Instead of vast emptiness, to find Jo in my bedroom when I came home from work each night? She smiled at me, and I forgot to breathe. I needed to say something, anything to break the silence. The window of opportunity to make her mine grew narrower as the seconds passed. We settled in the center of the enormous bed, the open pizza box between us, a nonsensical comedy playing on the television at low volume.

"I'm sorry about Harold," I said, choosing my words carefully. "I didn't know he'd be there."

"It's alright," she said through a mouthful of pepperoni pizza. "I kind of enjoyed the look on his face when he saw me, and especially when Calloway gave him his business card." Her smile lit up the room and my heart. "That was priceless."

"Yeah." Canned laughter echoed from the TV. Jo picked the pepperonis from her pizza slice and ate them one by one. We fell silent again. I became hyperaware of every blink of her eyes and nuance of her expression, dying to know what was happening inside her fascinating, pretty head.

"I'm sorry about your dad and the way everyone looked at you. I don't like him." The fingers of her left hand curled into a fist. "And

I'm on the fence about Reagan. Why would she invite you into that kind of environment unless she had an ulterior motive?"

I lowered my pizza to the plate and thought about her question. Why indeed? "We've known each other for about a year. She had no idea that I existed. I ran into her at a benefit for wounded soldiers last summer. I was there with Mom. Reagan put two and two together and figured it out. She said seeing me was like taking a trip back in time and meeting our father." I shook my head, remembering the way she'd cornered me and demanded answers. "Of course, I denied the connection, but she kept turning up at my office. That girl is like a bloodhound. Eventually, she hired a private detective and sniffed out the connection between my mom and the senator. He was really pissed." I snorted at the memory of his red-faced outrage.

"She probably used the truth to blackmail him. Apparently, that's a big thing in your family," Jo said between bites of food. I choked. She pounded my back until I found my breath again. "She over-shared *a lot* in the short time we talked. I can see why your dad is so big on non-disclosures."

"In his line of work, you can't be too careful. In fact, that's why he wanted to talk to me. He's worried you'll spill the family secrets to the press or the tabloids."

Her mouth, which had popped open, snapped shut again. She moistened her lips. "I'd never do that."

"I know. I trust you." Trust was a rare commodity in my world, something I didn't give lightly.

"You could always blackmail me to keep my mouth shut," she said, cocking a saucy eyebrow. "You know, family traditions and all."

"I can think of better uses for your mouth," I said, my gaze falling to her lips.

"A-a-a-nd he's back." She pushed her plate aside and groaned, patting her stomach, unfazed by my comment. "I ate too much."

"Am I fucking up again?" I asked, searching her face.

"No. I like that you say what you mean. Don't ever stop."

I moved the pizza and plates to the dresser and stretched out on the bed beside her. We stared at each other for a minute before Jo lowered to her side, facing me with her head propped on her hand. Blood thundered through my veins, spurred by the tender heat in her eyes. Usually, that kind of look would be my cue to burn rubber, but not this time. Not with her.

"About the other night, at the hotel, I should have told you about the warrant right away."

"That was a dick move, Eckhouse. I'm still a little pissed about it."

"I know, and you should be. My timing is bad. I don't have any experience with these things. I'm great with a pickup line, but I have no idea what happens after the sex part." She rolled her eyes, but a half smile played on her lips. "I want to find out—with you. I love you." The confession leaped from my heart to my mouth before my brain could censor it. A cold sweat sprang up on my forehead.

Her breath stuttered, breasts rising and falling, nipples plainly visible through my shirt. "Carter, I—"

"Before you say no, just listen." I blew out a deep breath and dove headlong into dangerous territory. I'd never been so nervous before. Then again, I'd never laid my heart out on a platter for anyone either. "I know you don't do relationships and neither do I, but what if we both agreed to not see anyone else—together, at the same time, with each other?"

"You really are bad at this," she said, and I couldn't decide if she was trying not to laugh or getting angry. "But keep going."

"That's it. That's all I've got." The saliva in my mouth had dried up, leaving my tongue fat and fuzzy. I cleared my throat, conscious of a scalding heat in my face. "Was it that bad?"

"No, it was sweet and perfect." She sat up, gathering her legs beneath her, and cupped my face, her touch light and tender.

"Is that a yes?"

"It's a maybe." Her pupils expanded, darkening her irises to black. "Before I can answer, I need to know, the other night, did you fuck someone else?"

With a thumb on her chin, I tipped her face to mine, searching, hoping to find the motive in her question. Did she have feelings for me? More than anything, I wanted her to be jealous. I wanted her to stake a claim on me. Rhett's words replayed in my head. *Being in a relationship isn't a nuisance, it's a privilege.* Now, I understood his point. I felt like I'd been gutted, my heart exposed and beating in the open air.

"When you came home late, I assumed—" The white edge of her upper teeth worried her pink bottom lip. "I just assumed you hooked up with someone."

Of course, she did, because that was my pattern. I prowled the bars looking for anonymous sex. Shame heated my face. I shoved it away, deep inside, to drag out and dissect at a later time. Right now, my skin itched. The kind of itch that only she could scratch. I opened my mouth to reply, but she stopped me with a finger to my lips.

"It's okay if you did. We weren't—aren't—together. But you need to know that when I'm with someone, I'm with them. I'm all in. I don't cheat. If we're together, I'll expect you to do the same."

I didn't want to get my hopes up, but this sounded promising. "I haven't been with anyone since this started between us." I hadn't even looked in the direction of another woman. Jo had been the only female on my mind. No one compared. No one.

"Because I can give you what you need, right?" Her hand smoothed down my abdomen and inside my sweats, fingers tightening around my erection, squeezing, punishing, demanding. I hissed at the pleasure-pain, enjoying her flirty tone as much as her confidence.

"Yes." I grunted. Lust tugged deep in my belly, contracting my balls. I cupped the left cheek of her bottom, letting my fingers dip into the tender flesh between her ass and her upper thigh.

"If I agree to be with you, I'll take care of you, Carter. I'll make sure you're satisfied in bed and everywhere else, but you have to treat me right." Her palm slid up my shaft. I swallowed and tried to speak. Nothing came out. When I met her gaze, she had a smirk, like she was enjoying my confusion. "No more withholding information. You have to be honest and upfront about everything, even if you think it'll upset me."

"I will. I promise." I held my breath, mesmerized when she bent, took my nipple ring between her teeth, and tugged.

"Okay, then." She pushed me onto the bed with more force than I thought possible for such a petite girl. "Just so you know, I'm in love with you too."

Using both hands, she drew the hem of the shirt over her head and tossed it aside. My heart skipped a beat at the sight of her flawless skin, the flat stretch of her belly, and the tiny triangle of her white cotton thong. I placed a hand on the small of her back, drawing her closer. The warmth of her bare back permeated my palm. With my free hand, I cupped one of her breasts, thumbing the tip until it jutted out.

"What am I going to do with you?" I asked, shaking my head. The ache in my balls escalated to a throb. "You're a handful."

"Shut up, Carter. You're talking too much," she said, right before she kissed me.

CHAPTER 26
JO

In the morning, I awoke to a heavy, male arm wrapped around my waist, and Carter's muscular chest glued against my back. Looking at him, naked and glorious, the bedsheets tangled around his narrow hips, made my heart race. He'd kept me close all night, pulling me into him, curling his body around mine. It was the best feeling in the world. I felt protected and cherished, like he truly appreciated my presence. Now that we were sort of, kind of seeing each other, I wasn't sure how to handle myself. I decided to take a shower and clean up before pondering all the changes in my life. The hot stream of water soothed my aching muscles and battered body. I closed my eyes and let myself relax for the first time in weeks. A knock on the bathroom door sent my heart into palpitations.

"Mind if I join you?" Carter's voice rumbled from outside the shower.

I peeked around the glass wall partition to find him standing in the center of the bathroom. "It's your shower. You don't need my permission."

A smirk curled his lips. He strode toward me, naked and confident. I bit my lower lip, mesmerized by the flat stretch of his belly, the cut of muscle below his hip bones, and the long, thick length of his cock between hard thighs. "You're like a fantasy come true," he said. His eyes darkened as they swept down the span of my nude body.

"So are you." I shivered at the heat in his eyes. He drew a fingertip down my sternum.

"If I asked you to get on your knees for me, would you?"

"Yes." I swallowed past the thickness in my throat. I kneeled in front of him, holding his hips. The granite tile bit into my knees, but I didn't care. This was erotic as hell. I'd kneel on broken glass if he asked me. He fisted a hand in the hair at my nape. Using the one hand, he tilted my face to look at him. I blinked against the spray of water at my back.

"Open." The pad of his thumb swept over my lip. Obediently, I opened my mouth, eager to taste the salt of his skin. With his free hand, he held the base of his cock. It jutted out, swollen and dark. His voice was harsh and broken. "Suck."

I did as he requested. Not because I owed him a dozen favors or because I felt intimidated. I did it because I wanted to give him pleasure. And I knew, without asking, that he'd give back more than I gave him, because that was the way he was.

With both hands gripping his ass for control, I let him fuck my mouth, slowly at first then in short, jabbing thrusts. The water beat down on my shoulders and back. The head of his cock brushed the back of my throat, bringing tears to my eyes. He threw his head back, braced one hand against the wall behind me, and groaned. When his legs began to shake, I knew he was close. I cupped a hand over his balls and kneaded. He began to plead and praise me in broken sentences. In that moment, I held all the power in our relationship.

"Oh God, don't stop. Please don't stop," he begged. "Jesus, your mouth. So sweet." He pushed into my throat. I gagged then swallowed, regaining control. He cursed as my muscles convulsed around him. "Fuck, you're good. That's it. Perfect. Don't stop. Deeper."

When the hot, salty taste of his release hit the back of my mouth, I smiled up at him. He smiled back, stroking a finger over my cheek. Our eyes met, and I came undone. I didn't want to have feelings for him, but I could no longer separate my desire from my emotions. There was something so tender and vulnerable in his touch. I blinked away tears of confusion. It was hard to remain distant when his eyes brimmed with heat and tenderness that matched my own.

He pulled me to my feet. Without a word, he poured a dollop of his shampoo into one of his palms and massaged it through my hair. I closed my eyes, enjoying the strength of his fingers on my scalp. Next, he took the loofah from its hook, loaded it with his shower gel, and began scrubbing my arms. I stood still and childlike, enjoying the attention. No part of my body escaped his attention. He took particular care between my legs. When I winced at the ache of his fingers on my tender flesh, he froze.

"Did I hurt you?"

"I'm a little bit sore from last night," I said, not wanting him to stop. "But it feels good."

"I rode you hard, didn't I?" It was more of a smug male statement than a question, so I didn't answer. He brushed his lips over my forehead. My pussy began to ache, this time from need. Screw the soreness. I wanted him again. I was beginning to wonder if I'd ever get enough of his big hands on my body or his ridiculously large penis inside me.

Once he'd finished washing me, I returned the favor. It gave me a chance to admire his body. I traced the thick veins running down his biceps, ran my palms over his smooth skin, pausing to tug on his nipple ring with my teeth. He grunted but didn't move. The twitch of his cock, hanging long and thick between his legs, told me he liked it a little rough. When I reached his ass, I bent down and bit his left cheek. He burst into laughter.

"What's that for?"

"You have the nicest ass I've ever seen."

"Well, that makes two of us," he said. He drew my front against his, cupping my bottom in his big hands. My chest swelled with love and lust. I rested my chin on his chest and blinked up at him. He brushed his fingers along my face, from temple to chin. "Damn, girl."

The confusing swell of emotions kicked up again. Standing like this, naked and vulnerable, seemed the most natural thing in the world and filled me with happiness. The warmth of his strong arms around me, the nudge of his cock against my belly, brought a contentment I'd never known before.

With a thick, fluffy towel, he dried me from head to toe. When he was finished, he tapped the tip of my nose with a finger. "Go lie on the bed. Knees up. Spread your legs wide."

"Why?" My hands shook as I pushed my damp hair away from my face.

"Don't ask questions." The smile slipped from his face. My belly flip flopped at the darkness in his tone. "I'm going to put my mouth here." He slipped a finger through my folds. I murmured in approval, pressing into his hand, already slick and needy. "I'm going to make this pussy mine."

CHAPTER 27

JO

A few weekends later, I came home from the coffee shop to find Carter and Rhett in the garage with my father. Their laughter carried all the way to the front yard. Dad wore a faded pair of blue jeans, a clean T-shirt, and an enormous smile. He greeted me with a hug.

"Hey, kiddo. How was work?" he asked.

"Fine. What's going on out here?" I studied the men suspiciously. In my limited experience, the three of them were mayhem in the making.

"We're working on the Olds," Dad said. "It's about time we got it up and running, don't you think?"

"Yes." I smiled back at him. The change in his appearance brought a lump to my throat. "I think it's a great idea."

"Hey." Carter emerged from underneath the hood and stalked toward me, a wrench in one hand. My mouth went dry at the sight of him and all those glorious muscles. He put his free hand on my ass, yanked my body against his, and ravaged my mouth with a long, deep kiss.

"Hey," I replied breathlessly once he let go. My head spun from the heat of his lips. I placed a hand on the wall until my balance returned.

"Did you have a good day?" His golden-brown eyes searched mine.

"Yes, but it's even better now." Everything seemed better with him around. We'd seen each other daily since the wedding. He came by the shop for coffee in the mornings, and he called or texted before bed each evening. In just a few short weeks, he'd integrated into my life until I couldn't imagine going a full day without him.

Rhett grinned at us over the top of the car.

"What's wrong with him?" I asked Carter.

"Don't mind me," Rhett said, his face turning deep red from a buildup of suppressed laughter. "But apparently this is the day that hell freezes over."

"I'll alert the media," Dad said dryly, but he was smiling too.

"Knock it off, Easton, Mr. H," Carter growled, but his eyes softened as he pressed a kiss to my forehead. "Ignore them." I beamed up at him, enjoying the dynamic playing out between the men. He smoothed a hand down my back. "I picked up a little something for you today. It's in the house. Why don't you go get it?"

"Okay." I narrowed my eyes at him, mindful of his penchant for mischief. "What is it?"

"Just go look." One corner of his mouth curled up in the playful smirk I'd come to love.

After a shrug, I crossed the backyard and climbed the steps to the kitchen stoop. When I opened the door, a ball of white fur flashed past my legs. Chaos erupted inside my chest. Zipper yipped and yelped, licking my ankles, squirming and wiggling in canine ecstasy.

"Zipper! Oh, my goodness. Come here, buddy," I said, my voice breaking with emotion. He leaped into my arms, bestowing furious kisses on my chin. "Good boy." Tears burned the back of my throat. I glanced around for Carter. He stood beside me. Dad and Rhett hovered in the background. "Who— What— How did you do this?"

He shrugged, eyes sparkling. "I paid your boyfriend a visit today.

I took a few of my guys with me. Harold was more than happy to hand over your dog once we had a little discussion."

"He's not my boyfriend." With Zipper tucked under my arm, I placed my free hand on Carter's stubbled cheek. "You're my boyfriend."

"Damn straight," he replied, his smile widening.

Our eyes met. An overwhelming rush of contentment swept through me from head to toe. My feelings had escalated from lust to love while I hadn't been looking. I still wanted him more than anything in the world, but our bond went deeper than physical desire. I trusted him, and I knew without a doubt, that he'd never intentionally hurt me.

In a voice too low for anyone's ears but his, I said, "You're getting fucked within an inch of your life tonight."

"Yes!" He wrapped an arm around my waist and escorted me back to the garage. Zipper sniffed and cavorted at our heels. I couldn't take my eyes off the dog or my boyfriend. It was too good to be true. But this was my new reality, and I meant to enjoy every minute of it.

"I think we should have a toast," Dad said, handing me a beer. The four of us lifted our bottles. "To Zipper, the little bastard. He'd better not shit in my shoes like he used to. And to Carter. I knew the minute you came to the door that you'd be the one to tame my little princess. Welcome to the family, son. I hope you stick around a while."

"Me too." I spoke the words aloud before I realized what I'd said. Carter blinked, his expression sobering. Panic chilled my veins. The last thing I wanted was to scare him off by being too clingy or needy. "I mean—"

He pressed a finger to my lips. "Stop talking, Hollander. I'm not going anywhere."

EPILOGUE
CARTER

For the tenth time in the space of an hour, I patted my pockets. One year ago, on this very date, I'd tackled Clarence Mortimer Benson III in Joe's Java Junction and found the love of my life. My breathing stuttered. "Shit. I think I lost the ring," I said, my voice high and broken like a boy in puberty.

"It's right here, buddy," Rhett said. He lifted his hand, where Jo's wedding band encircled his little finger. "Calm down. You're going to stroke out before we get to the judge."

"I'm okay." I closed my eyes and tried to breathe through the panic.

"You'll be fine. I promise." His mirthful tone forced me to open my eyes. "You can always call the whole thing off. You can sneak out the side door. I'll go tell Jo."

"No way. Are you fucking nuts?" Hearing his teasing words put the world into perspective. This was my wedding day. In a few short minutes, I'd be exchanging vows with the girl of my dreams. Nothing short of a zombie apocalypse could tear me away from her side.

"Excellent. The girls are waiting. Let's get this show on the road." He opened the door of the men's room and flourished a hand. "After you." We took two strides into the hallway before he stopped. "Wait. I forgot something."

"Jesus Christ, Easton. You're killing me here," I growled. "Now what?" The serious glint of his eyes tied my guts in knots. "You lost the ring, didn't you? Fuck."

He placed a hand on my shoulder and squeezed. "I just want to say I'm proud of you, man. Really proud." His voice broke a little on the last word. He cleared his throat. "I never thought I'd see this day. Thank you for letting me witness this amazing event." The mischief returned to his eyes. "And also, back in eighth grade, you made a bet with me that you'd never get married. I'll expect you to deliver your ten-speed bike to my apartment by the end of the week."

"Dick," I said, feeling my throat close with emotion. I pretended to punch him in the abs. "As I recall, you borrowed that bike and never gave it back."

"Oh, yeah. Right." He shrugged then paused to straighten my tie. "My bad."

We pushed through the doors together. Jo stood on the other side, pale and anxious. There were other people in the room, but I only had eyes for her. Sunlight glinted off the brown waves of her hair, worn loose especially for me. Her lips curved into a smile at the sight of me, her complexion warming as I got closer.

"Hey," I said.

"Hey." She smiled up at me with enormous blue eyes, glassy with unshed tears.

"Why are you shaking?" The leaves of her simple bouquet trembled violently. I stroked a finger over the curve of her cheek, a herd of butterflies pinging around in my stomach. Maybe she was having second thoughts. "Are you scared?"

"No, I thought you might change your mind."

"No way. You're never getting rid of me." I gave her a wink. "Not without a court order, anyway."

After the judge pronounced us man and wife, I kissed Jo and took her hand in mine. We turned in unison to face our witnesses. Bronte beamed at us. Rhett gave me a high-five and kissed Jo on the cheek. Mr. H shook my hand effusively until I thought my arm would fall off. And Darcy sobbed throughout the entire ten-minute ceremony.

On the courthouse steps, Darcy leaned in to give me a hug. "I'm so happy for you, Carter. You deserve this."

"Thanks." I squeezed her hand, grateful for her friendship.

My mother, expecting a visit from the senator, hadn't even bothered to respond to the invitation, but I was okay with it. She had her life to live, and I had mine. Someday, when the senator tired of her, I'd be there to pick up the pieces. In the meantime, I had a new family to call my own, and the love of my life to thank for them.

Thank you for reading *Pretty Broken Bastard*. If this is your first book in the Pretty Broken Series, go back to the beginning with this **FREE** read.

Pretty Broken Girl

1100+ 5-star ratings on Goodreads

"Original! This broken romance tugs at your heartstrings!" —Bookbub Reviewer

A divorced couple battles for control in the boardroom but things heat up when their competition reaches the bedroom.

Ten years ago, I divorced the love of my life for all the wrong reasons. I had no idea he'd walk through my office door ten years later as my new boss, more handsome than ever, determined to make me pay for my sins. My knees go weak every time I look at him. Too bad he hates me. He's determined to make my life hell. The only thing I know for sure? We can still heat up the sheets. He thinks he can break me, but I'm not the girl I was.

From the bedroom to the boardroom, Sam and Dakota are locked in a battle of wits and desire. One of them will break. One of them will pay. Both of them want to win. Neither of them expects to fall in love—again.

You'll never look at a closed office door the same way again. GET IT HERE>>>Pretty Broken Girl

---

NEED MORE? Here's a preview of THE EXILED PRINCE, a billionaire, royalty romance.

THE EXILED PRINCE

Rourke

I wandered through the ballroom, mesmerized by the scores of beautiful people. Behind their masks lurked some of the most famous faces in the world. Every now and then, I thought I recognized the curve of a woman's smile or the width of a man's shoulders, but I had no way of knowing who was who. The masks came in all shapes and sizes. Some were elaborate combinations of feathers and gems on a background of satin. Others were sleek and simple like Ivan's. Everly had picked up my mask on one of her many trips to Venice. It rested lightly above my nose, held in place by strings of silk, allowing a clear view of my eyes but obscuring enough to hide my identity.

After a few minutes, I began to grow comfortable among the guests and had to admit I was enjoying the anonymity. Without the threat of disapproval, I could do anything, and be anyone, I wanted.

A brown-haired man in a navy tuxedo tapped my arm. "I was wondering if you'd like to dance?"

Remembering my promise to Everly, I accepted. His aristocratic features and pleasant smile bolstered my resolve to meet someone new. "I might be a little rusty. I haven't danced in years. If you don't mind my clumsy feet, then I don't mind either."

He extended a hand. "It's my pleasure."

I placed my hand in his and let him lead me to the dance floor. The brush of our palms together sent a pleasant ripple along my skin. The orchestra segued smoothly from a foxtrot into a waltz. From the sidelines, Everly nodded approvingly. My heart skipped a beat when he put his arm around my waist. It felt good to be held by a man again. He twirled me around the floor until I was breathless, ignoring the many times I stepped on the toes of his shiny shoes.

At the end of the song, he smiled down at me with full lips and gray bedroom eyes. Beneath the dark blue velvet mask lurked the face of a handsome man, around my age, maybe younger. "That was delightful. You've made my evening."

"Thank you. You're too kind." I smiled. He lifted my hand to his lips, grazing his mouth over my knuckles, sending a shiver of attraction through my body. "You can call me Nicky. And what should I call you?"

Panic evaporated the moisture from my mouth. I cleared my throat. "I thought we weren't supposed to reveal our real names."

"I never said it was my real name." He watched me closely, waiting for my answer, his gaze focused on my lips.

"You can call me—" I searched for an appropriate name. "You can call me Cinderella."

His burst of laughter escalated my panic. "Oh, that's priceless.

Well, Cinderella, tell me, how did you come by an invitation to the elusive Masquerade de Marquis?"

I tried to smile and stay calm, deflecting the question with one of my own. If I'd learned anything during my years with Everly, it was that people loved to talk about themselves. "I kind of fell into it." Not exactly a lie but not the truth, either. "What about you? Have you attended to the masquerade before?" I kept walking in the direction of the ladies' powder room, preparing to excuse myself before I got into trouble.

"A few times." He fell into step beside me. "No one turns away an invitation unless they want to offend the host, and Mr. Menshikov doesn't like to be offended." His eyes watched me with the sharpness of a hawk watching a mouse. The predatory nature of his stare raised the tiny hairs on my arms.

"Are you a celebrity?" I kept my tone light and teasing but cast a glance in the direction of the ladies' room, judging the distance.

"In some circles." A dimple popped on his right cheek. "Mostly I'm here because I have friends in high places."

"Are you a friend of Mr. Menshikov?" My sense of self-preservation went to war with my curiosity. I wanted to know more about the enigmatic host without giving too much of myself in return.

"Friends?" The sharpness in his laugh made me flush. Obviously, I'd crossed an invisible boundary. "Roman doesn't have friends."

"Ivan said he's not here tonight." I stopped walking and gave my full attention to Nicky, hoping to coax more information from him. "Do you know him? Roman, I mean?"

"I don't think anyone truly knows Roman." Mystery edged his words. Mistaking my curiosity for the host as interest in him personally, he smiled and took my hand again. He lifted it to look at the ring on my little finger. Delicate strands of silver and gold vines twisted together to form a circle. Amethysts sprinkled throughout the band like tiny flowers. "Your ring—it's very unique."

"It belonged to my mother," I said, running my thumb over it. "My father had it made for her when I was born."

"Ah, how romantic." He stroked the band with a fingertip, the light pressure tickling along my skin. "Speaking of romantic, would you like to take a walk in the garden? There are all kinds of entertainers down there. There's nothing I love more than a moonlight stroll with a beautiful woman." He leaned down, his tone lowering. "Someone said there are naked performers dancing through fire. How can you pass up a chance to see something like that?"

Although his charm was infectious, I shrank away from the opportunity. I didn't want to blow my cover. A few yards away, Everly lifted an eyebrow. Although she didn't speak, I knew her well enough to understand the message. *Get your ass out there. Live a little.*

I squared my shoulders. "Thank you so much for the invitation, but I think I'd like to dance some more." Dancing was safe. With the music swelling and the hum of conversation and laughter surrounding us, there was little opportunity for questions I didn't want to answer.

"Fair enough." He bent low in a deep bow. "May I have the honor of this dance?"

For the next several hours, I danced with Nicky until my feet ached, drank champagne until my head swam, and laughed until my insides quivered. He was delightful, although his prodding questions required my skillful avoidance.

"Who is that man?" I asked, having caught sight of a gentleman near the fireplace, his forearm resting on the mantle. Although I couldn't see his eyes behind his mask, I felt the weight of his relentless gaze following us around the room as we danced. The curling edges of his dark hair hung to his collar, its messiness at odds with the crisp lines of his tuxedo.

"Where?" Nicky followed the incline of my head. "Oh." For the first time, he missed a step. His shoulders tensed beneath my touch, the smile sliding from his face before he recovered. "I'm not sure. He could be anyone."

Was it my imagination, or had I heard a touch of Russian accent in Nicky's reply? "He keeps staring at us."

"Probably because you're so beautiful," Nicky said. In an adept maneuver, he directed us toward the opposite end of the room. Within minutes, I forgot about the stranger, too focused on following Nicky's lead and the heady exhilaration of being held by such a charismatic guy.

"It's getting late, and I have to leave soon," he said, leading me toward the row of chairs along the wall. "I know it's against the rules, but I can't go without learning your name—your real name."

"You know I can't tell you that," I said, still breathless from his touch and the physical exertion.

"But you can. It's just a stupid rule Roman invented for his own amusement. You can tell me. No one has to know." He squeezed my hand tighter, his jaw tightening. "I want to see you again."

"No. You can't." At the flicker of hurt in his eyes, I softened my refusal. After all, he seemed like a nice guy. "There's no point."

"You're married?" His grip loosened on my fingers.

"No, no, nothing like that. It's just that I'm going back to America in a few days." Behind his mask, his eyes searched mine. I fisted my hands, resisting the urge to brush his light brown hair from his forehead.

"I travel to the States frequently. I could look you up. We could have dinner, and you could show me the sights."

"Excuse me, may I cut in?" A smooth, deep voice sliced into our conversation. From his accent, he was American, a New Yorker or somewhere on the east coast.

Nicky and I both turned to face the stranger. A black leather mask prevented me from going further than the curve of full, pouting lips. My gaze traveled from the onyx buttons of his charcoal vest down the perfect crease of his dark gray trousers to the shiny, pointed toes of his black shoes. Unlike the other formally attired guests, the tail of his silver bow tie dangled from the breast pocket of his jacket. The lack of formality seemed out of place and rebellious in a room overflowing with perfection.

"We were having a conversation," Nicky said, his tone acidic. The change in his demeanor caught me by surprise. I glanced from him to the stranger. A palpable air of animosity pulsed between them.

"Watch your manners, Nicky." The stranger's light rebuke reminded me of a parent scolding a rebellious child. "Please forgive him. He's been running with the wolves for too long."

"At least I'm still running." There was no mistaking the competitive edge in his words.

My gaze bounced between the two men. Whatever their relationship, it was complicated and intriguing.

"Not here. Not now. Not in front of our lovely companion." While he spoke, his dark eyes locked onto mine. He took my hand in his long, graceful fingers, his smooth palm gliding against mine, and lifted my knuckles to his mouth. My heart stopped at the brush of his soft lips on my skin. In the background, the introduction to a tango began. "Dance with me."

Three words sent my pulse into overdrive. "The tango used to be my favorite, but I haven't done it in years." I panicked at the thought of the intricate moves.

"Don't worry. I'll take care of everything." After another kiss to my knuckles, he led me to the center of the dance floor. The guests parted, making way for us, their eyes heavy on my back. I couldn't blame their stares. This man exuded confidence, elegance, and power. He placed my left hand on his waist and took the right in his palm. Shying away from his gaze, I stared at his throat. The top two buttons of his crisp white shirt gaped open, revealing a triangle of smooth, tanned skin dusted with black hair. He squeezed my hand, demanding my attention. "Eyes to mine. Don't look at your feet. Follow my lead."

Behind the mask, his eyes were dark, almost black. Anxiety closed my throat. This would either be an amazing experience or extremely embarrassing. Probably the latter. The music swelled, and we began. Within a few steps, I captured his rhythm. He was strong and forceful, moving me into each position, twirling me out then snapping me back against his chest. I gasped at the press of my breasts against hard muscles.

"Very nice," he said. A neatly trimmed beard and moustache couldn't obscure a square jaw, reminding me of a jaunty pirate.

"Thank you." The warmth of his approval spread through my chest.

"I'm going to have to step up my game." His eyes glittered with challenge.

"Yes. You are." They were bold words for a girl who hadn't danced the tango in six years, but I didn't care. I liked the feel of his body against mine and the strength in his arms. More than anything, I enjoyed the way his overpowering maleness made me feel feminine and dainty.

"Be careful what you ask for." His arms tightened around me. I slid slowly down his torso and pressed my breasts into the hard lines of his body. When my eyes reached the level of his narrow hips, he yanked me to my feet. The crowd gasped.

"You surprise me," he said.

"You aren't the only one with secrets, sir." The hem of my skirt swirled around my ankles. The slit opened to flash a stretch of my leg and the white garter belt around my thigh. I felt his gaze go there. It returned to mine, flashing with desire.

"So, I see." By the humor in his tone, my answer pleased him. Or maybe it was the garter. There was no more time for conversation as the intensity of the music continued to escalate.

This was more than a dance. It was a test. A game of dominance and submission underscored by sexual tension. I stiffened my arms and pulled away. The words of my dance instructor floated through my subconscious. *Be angry. Let the audience see the struggle.* He snapped my body to his and stroked a leisurely hand from my armpit to my hip. Goosebumps peppered my skin. I spun away, only to be returned by a tug of his arm. We continued our war of wills around the room.

At the finale, he bent me backward over his thigh, arching my spine until the ends of my hair swept the floor. The smooth fabric of his trousers rubbed against my bare back. I was totally at his mercy, one foot on the polished marble, the other lifted to keep from tumbling over. His lips grazed the column of my throat in an erotic caress. Excitement and lust simmered in my veins. I was living my fantasies in the arms of an exotic stranger.

The music ended, and the crowd erupted into applause. I'd been so engrossed in our power play that I'd failed to notice the onlookers, or that all the other participants had moved to the sidelines. We were the only couple on the dance floor. Under normal circumstances, this kind of attention would have made my stomach queasy, but beside him, it seemed natural.

Adrenalin buzzed through my head, more intoxicating than the liquor. He eased me to my feet. Once I'd steadied myself, he released my hand and bowed. "Thank you for the dance." Before I could respond, he melted into the crowd. I watched his broad shoulders disappear. A curious sense of regret tempered my euphoria. That was it? One amazing dance, and he left?

Someone touched my elbow. I erased the disappointment from my expression and turned to find Everly. She drew me aside and fanned her cheeks with a cocktail napkin. "Holy crap, Rourke. That was hot. Who is that man?"

"I'm not sure." I stared wistfully in the direction he'd gone, but my attention wavered at the weight of Nicky's disapproving stare on the stranger's backside. What was it between those two men? "I think he's Roman Menshikov."

Everly's gaze followed mine in the direction the stranger had gone. Her brows lowered. "It could be, but I don't think so. Everyone says he's out of the country."

"I know, but there's something about him." I searched through the guests, looking for disheveled black hair and an unshaven jaw.

"Did you ask him?"

"How could I? I certainly can't tell him who I am. Ivan will throw me out."

"True. Well, no matter. You have another admirer," Everly said, her eyes dancing with delight, nodding toward Nicky. "This is so exciting. Are you having a good time?"

"Yes." The answer required no conscious thought. "I haven't had this much fun in years." As always, my thoughts returned to her welfare. "What about you?"

"I'm having a great time. A few of my friends are here." She squeezed my hand. "Thank you so much for coming. I could never have attended on my own. This is the best bachelorette night ever."

"You're welcome. Thank you for dragging me here." I smiled back at her, thrilled by her excitement.

"I think you should hook up with one of those men." The mischievous glint returned to her eyes. "A good lay would do wonders for your self-confidence."

"Oh, no." I shook my head.

"Yes. You absolutely should. Think about it. Everyone here is anonymous. It's like Las Vegas. What happens here, stays here." Her eyebrows lifted, but she quickly got her expression under control and ducked her head. "Don't look now, but the brown-haired gentleman is coming this way, and he doesn't seem happy." She waggled her eyebrows. "Look at you, stirring the shit. I'm out of here. Have fun and be safe."

"Don't you dare leave me, Everly." Despite my plea, she sashayed toward the back hall, waving her fingers over her shoulder in my direction. "Traitor." I steeled myself for more of Nicky's questions.

"Did you enjoy your dance?" he asked.

I hope you enjoyed this look at The Exiled Prince, Book 1 of The Exiled Prince Trilogy. It was written as a standalone, and has a happy-for-now ending. It's FREE everywhere! You can start reading here...THE EXILED PRINCE

Intoxicated
Unexpected
Vindicated
Impulsive
Drift
Committed

BAD BEHAVIOR SERIES
(Releasing in 2020 and 2021)

Bad Behavior #1
Bad Behavior #2
Bad Behavior #3
Bad Behavior #4
Bad Behavior #5

STANDALONES
Lies We Tell
Dirty Work

SHORT STORIES
Everything
Linger

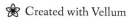 Created with Vellum

BONUS SHORT STORY

1

HARDER

ROMEO

The woman beneath me moans. I press deeper into her soft, wet heat. Her hips jerk upward, wanting more, needing more, and I aim to give it to her. With three thrusts, I take her to the edge and hold her there. She's close, so close, and so am I. The bite of her fingernails stings down my back. I hiss as my balls tighten and fight the burning need to climax, because this isn't about me. This is about her—her needs, her desires, her fantasies.

"Harder, Romeo."

Her use of my professional name throws off my rhythm. My clients call me Romeo, but to everyone else, I'm Jamie. I've found it best to keep my real name private. Less messy, and absolutely necessary in case one of my clients forms an obsession. I had the misfortune of dealing with a stalker once, and ever since then, I've used an alias to protect my anonymity. "Any harder and your headboard is going to knock a hole in the wall."

"I don't care." The raw edge to her voice tells me everything I need to know about her state of mind.

"Jesus, you're tight today." I double the pace, driving my pelvis into her like a jackhammer. Another fiery pulse of release licks up the back of my legs. I try to think about something other than shooting my load. The faulty starter on my car. The potential negative balance in my bank account. My pace begins to slow under the negative thoughts, so I shift the tone to more pleasant topics. *Baseball.* Always a winner. In my head, I run through the names and stats of the Cubs starting lineup. The fire in my groin fades to a mild simmer. My thoughts drift from baseball to cars, and now I'm hot again. She tightens her slender thighs around my waist. Damn. If she doesn't get off soon, I'm going to bust a nut before she does, and that just can't happen.

"I'm almost there," she warns. Her tits bounce with every slam of my body against hers.

"I know you are, baby. So am I." With a huge amount of effort, I withdraw. We both groan in frustration. I flip her over onto her knees, fist a hand in her hair, and shove into her hard enough to make her grunt. A shudder ripples through her body and clutches around my cock. I ride out her orgasm, waiting until her cries die down, then spill into the condom between us. The relief is immediate—thank God—because I'm not sure how much longer I could hold off.

After a few seconds, we break apart and roll onto our backs, chests heaving, covered in sweat. I remove the condom, tie it off, and drop it onto the floor next to my shoes to take care of later. Blood still thunders through my veins. I close my eyes and try to regulate my breathing. Beside me, I hear the flick of a lighter and the sizzle of flame against the tip of a cigarette. Ms. Denney inhales, holds it for a second, then exhales slowly.

"I'm getting married next week," she says.

"Oh?" My eyes snap open. She's been a regular for over a year. I'll need to fill her spot with someone new.

"Yes." She sits up, holding the sheet over her breasts. Her shoulder-length, silver hair stands out around her head, tangled by my clutching fingers. Intelligent blue eyes meet mine. She hands me her cigarette. I take a long drag and hand it back. "But nothing is going to change between you and me. He lives on the west coast. I'll be here. We can continue like usual."

"A long-distance marriage? Really?" A smile tugs my lips. "How's that going to work? You're in Chicago. He's there. Sounds difficult." As a flawed human being, I try not to judge, but I know one thing for damn sure. If I get married, I'll take my vows seriously. I'll never cheat, and I'll move the stars above to make sure she's satisfied inside *and* outside of the bedroom. When the guilt becomes too great, I justify sleeping with married women by telling myself that if they're going to cheat, it might as well be with a single dad who needs to support his baby girl.

"It's going to work great." She smiles back, and I'm struck by her beauty. Even though she's a good thirty years older than I am, she's one hell of a woman. Long legs, nice rack. "He has a corporation in San Francisco and comes here on business a couple of times a month. This way, we enjoy the tax and social benefits of marriage, while maintaining our individual lives."

"Nice." I sit up, drop my legs over the edge of the bed, and let my toes curl into the sheepskin rug beneath my feet. The room is monochromatic, minimalist, with a few luxurious touches here and there. A wall of windows displays a panoramic view of Chicago from the sixtieth floor of the skyscraper. Someday, I'll have a place like this instead of a shitty one-bedroom apartment. "I'm going to take a shower. Care to join me?"

"No. Go ahead. I've got a few things to take care of." She stubs out the cigarette in an ashtray on the nightstand and grabs her laptop.

When I come out of the shower, she's wearing a set of silver silk pajamas. The thin fabric outlines a figure taut from exercise, a body I know as well as my own. I walk across the room, naked, knowing she likes to watch me, and dress slowly in front of her.

"We'll have to skip the next few weeks," she says, her tone matter-of-fact. "But we can pick up our regular schedule after the honeymoon."

"Okay. Works for me." In truth, I can use a little time off. The last few months have been a shitshow of personal drama. However, I'd be lying if I said the loss of income won't hurt my situation. I bend to drop a kiss on her cheek. One of her hands slips an envelope, my payment, into the back pocket of my jeans and something else, something bulky. I reach into my pocket and draw out a set of car keys dangling from a gold fob. "What's this?"

"It's a little something extra for you, for being so sweet." The fingertips of her left hand trail over my ass, ending in a pat.

I narrow my eyes. She's always been generous to a fault, but this —this is new. "You're lending me your car?"

"No, I'm *giving* you a car." An indulgent smile curves her lips.

"I can't take this." Payment for sex is one thing, a car is entirely different. It's too permanent, too tangible. I hand the keys back to her.

"Don't be ridiculous." She shoves my hand aside. "It's yours, darling. Free and clear." As the founder and president of an all-female law firm, she's used to giving commands and being obeyed. "Take the damn car. Enjoy it. Life is too short." Her voice softens, and so does the hardness in her eyes. "The last year would've been unbearable without you. You've earned it."

I don't mean to brag, but I'm good at what I do, and I take pride in my skills. I have a natural head for business, and I'm great in the sack. Combining the two assets only seems natural. Women crave a good fuck. Not awkward fumbling under the sheets or a quick grope and poke. They want ball-slapping, headboard-banging, finger-clutching sex. Turns out, they're also happy to pay for it.

I squeeze the keys. Hell, I'm no fool. My pride smarts for an entire thirty seconds, but the sting disappears the minute I enter the parking garage. A cobalt blue, sleek and shiny, Lexus sits in a reserved space on the ground floor. It's the most beautiful thing I've ever seen —next to a woman's face when she comes. I trail my fingertips over the glossy paint and sink into the buttery leather seat with a moan of hedonistic pleasure. Once I'm behind the steering wheel, I take the envelope from my back pocket and thumb through the crisp hundred dollar bills. Not bad for two hours of work.

It's hard to believe that two years ago, I was penniless, on the verge of a nervous breakdown, and damn near suicidal. Today, at the tender age of twenty-four, it feels like I've got the world by the ass, and I've got to tell you—it doesn't suck.

A few days later, I'm in the gym at my apartment building. The girl on the treadmill next to mine gives me an admiring sideways glance. I punch up the speed and ignore the slide of her gaze over my body. I run for thirty minutes. She matches my pace. I'm impressed. Not a bad looking girl, although she's probably forty pounds overweight. To be clear, size doesn't matter to me. In fact, I prefer a nice, round ass with some bounce to it, like hers. And don't get me started on her tits. Their round tops jiggle inside a snug, pink athletic bra. Nice. If I hadn't just finished up a night of fucking, I'd be all over that. But I'm tired, my refrigerator is empty, and I need to pick up my dry cleaning after the workout.

At the end of my run, I stop the machine and hop off, pausing to wipe down the surfaces. She heads to the water fountain for a drink of water. A few minutes later, we board the elevator together. She stands a little in front of me and gets off at the fourth floor. I continue up to the twentieth floor where I shower, change clothes, and drink a protein shake before heading to the street.

When I come out of the building, she's waiting by the curb for a taxi. The short skirt of her dress flutters in the breeze. She shoots me a smile, and I smile back, because that's the kind of guy I am —friendly.

"Heading to work?" she asks. Her voice is sweet, melodic, tainted with innocence.

I shake my head. "Running errands."

"I'm Chloe." She extends a hand, and I take it. Her grip is surprisingly firm and warm.

"Nice to meet you." I don't give her my name. Names only lead to trouble.

"Do you have time for a coffee? I'm not due at work for another hour." Round, hopeful eyes lock on mine.

I stare back at her, feeling like a wolf in the presence of a sacrificial lamb. She has no idea who I am or what I do. The sinner inside me wants to accept her offer, but the saint draws rein. I've been down this street before, and it leads to heartbreak—for her. I glance at my watch. "I don't—"

"There's a place around the corner to the left, I think." She tucks a strand of brown hair behind her small, pink ear.

"It's that way." I point in the opposite direction.

"Oh. Right." Twin patches of red bloom in her cheeks. "I just moved here a few weeks ago. I still can't find my way around."

In spite of my reservations, I can't help smiling at her wholesome appeal. She's a refreshing change of pace. My clients are middle-aged women, often married, and always jaded by life. Work keeps me too busy for meeting people of my own age. Until now, I had no idea how much I'd missed my friends.

"I keep getting lost. The city—it's so big. I'm from a small town in Indiana, you know? Chicago is on a completely different playing field than my hometown." I lift an eyebrow, and her blush deepens. "That was way too much information, wasn't it? I'm sorry." She rolls her eyes, and I fight the urge to laugh at her cuteness.

"No worries. See ya around." From my jeans pocket, my phone vibrates. I send the call to voicemail then give Chloe a farewell nod. I don't want to be rude, but past experience has taught me to walk away before the conversation becomes too personal.

"See ya," she calls after me. I can feel her gaze burning on my backside, and it causes a funny twinge in my gut. To curb the urge to glance at her over my shoulder, I focus on the parking garage. My heart beats a little faster at the sight of the glossy paint of my new ride. Once I'm behind the wheel, I listen to the voice message on the car's handsfree system and exit the garage. It's Miranda, my first Jane, the woman who started my career as a manwhore.

I hit redial, watching Chloe through the windshield. She tries without success to flag down two consecutive cabs. Her shoulders droop. I bump up the volume on the phone call, unable to tear my gaze away from her.

"Good morning, Romeo," Miranda purrs. "How's my boy this morning?"

"Great. How are you?" As I run a finger around the leather stitching of the steering wheel, Chloe hops up and down on the curb, waving at an approaching taxi like a mad woman. I chuckle at her enthusiasm.

"Honey, if I got any better, it would be illegal." Miranda's cultured voice washes over me. "But enough about me, I'm calling because I have a friend who'd like to meet you."

"Cool. Appreciate it." Good old Miranda. Not only did she save me from going to jail a few years ago, she's responsible for half my clients. Without her, I'd still be selling weed from a bench in Garfield Park. "And you'll vouch for her?" A guy in my line of work can't be too careful.

"I've known her for years. Her husband's a senator. Believe me, she'll die before she tells a soul about you."

For an instant, the world spins at the prospect of such a high-level client. I recover and find my voice. "She's down with the terms?"

"Of course."

"It might be a few weeks. My schedule is full." I frown at the red appointment squares on my calendar app. Working as a personal trainer is becoming more of a hassle than a necessity. My earnings as a manwhore far exceed the paltry salary of training, but the lesser job provides a legitimate income for tax purposes. I don't need the IRS asking questions about my business.

"I'd consider it a personal favor if you could work her in." She hesitates before speaking again. "Her husband is out of town on business. If you do this, she'll be very, *very* grateful."

In other words, there will be a bonus for my inconvenience. "Okay. I'll see what I can do."

"Oh dear, I'm late for court. I'll see you Thursday." She hangs up, and I punch in the new prospect's number.

"Hello?" A woman answers on the second ring.

"Hi, I'm calling for Mrs. Smith." Most women don't give their real names in order to protect their privacy. I've got a dozen Mrs. Smiths on my client roster. "Miranda gave me your number."

"Yes." The voice is soft-spoken, has a Texas drawl, and shakes a little. Obviously, she's nervous. She clears her throat and whispers, "Are you—the personal trainer?"

"Yep." That's me. Manwhore. Gigolo. Escort. I'm all those things and then some. "Is this a bad time to talk? Would you like me to call back?"

"No, no. Now is fine." I hear the frown in her voice. From her tone and style of speaking, I'd peg her for an unhappily married woman in her forties. Probably got a few kids, husband works all the time, looking for a little male attention. "Are you available tonight?"

"Sure. Tonight's fine." I've been looking forward to a night off, but the loss of Ms. Denney's income over the next few weeks has me rethinking my financial situation. "Do you have any questions about the process?"

"No. I understand. My friend explained everything." The woman draws in a deep breath and exhales. "Can you come over, say around nine?"

"Sounds perfect. Is there anything specific you're looking for?"

"No. I don't think so." Embarrassment is obvious in her tone. "I like—I like it a little rough. Not mean, just forceful. Is that okay?"

"Sure. No problem. I'll give it to you any way you like." Because customer service is number one in my book. I smirk, thinking of all the ways I've done women in the past. After two years of turning tricks, nothing surprises me anymore. *Nothing.*

"What do you look like?" Curiosity replaces her nervousness. "Miranda—she said you're sexy. I just wondered..."

"I'm six-four, a hundred and eighty pounds, dark hair, brown eyes, a trimmed beard. I work out every day, and I'm in excellent shape." These kinds of questions don't bother me. I'm not cheap, and she has every right to make sure she's getting her money's worth. "And in case you're wondering, I've got plenty of horsepower under the hood. Enough to keep you satisfied all night."

The woman gives me her address. I enter the appointment into my phone. When I look up, raindrops splatter on the windshield. Chloe is still standing on the curb, her purse lifted over her head to fend off the rain. Oh, what the hell. I can't leave the girl out in the elements, can I? I ease the car up to the curb in front of her and roll down the window. "Get in. I can drop you."

"Um, are you sure?" She rolls her lips together then tugs the lower one between her teeth. "You're not a serial killer or anything, are you?"

I open the passenger door and wait for her to hop inside. "Not even close."

THANKS FOR THE RIDE

After Chloe gives me the address to her office, we drive in silence for the next block. She smells like citrus and honey, a lethal combination. Her scent fills the cockpit of the Lexus, mingling with the new car smell. While I drive, she lowers the visor and peers into the mirror to smooth her hair.

"This is a nice car," she says. One of her hands caresses the soft leather covering the console. "What did you say you do?"

"I'm a personal trainer."

Her sideways gaze cuts to the swell of my biceps, and a blush creeps into her cheeks. "You're a walking billboard for fitness."

"Thanks." My body is the tool that keeps a roof over my head, food in my refrigerator, and clothes on my back. I treat it like a temple because it is.

"I wish I had your self-discipline." She sighs. "No matter what I do, I can't seem to lose any weight."

"I think you look great just the way you are, but if you're looking for guidance, you should come to one of my training sessions. I offer nutritional counseling and a realistic workout plan to maximize calorie burn." The offer pops out of my mouth before I can stop it. So much for keeping my professional and personal lives separate. I press my lips together before I do something stupid like offer to fuck her for free.

"Really? That would be great. Maybe I'll take you up on that." She flips the visor up and shifts to face me. "Did you go to school for that?"

I try not to gawk at the smooth skin of her bare legs. She's curvy in all the right places, and I have an inexplicable urge to put my hand on her thigh. Instead, I curl my fingers around the gear shift. "Indiana University at Bloomington." I completed three years before I blew out my elbow, lost my baseball scholarship, and moved back home to Chicago. It seems like a lifetime ago—another life entirely. "I never finished my degree, though."

"You must be doing really well to afford a car like this. I'm barely making enough for rent. This city is so expensive. Of course, my grandmother wants me to live with her, but I said no way." She pauses for breath, and I have to laugh at her genuine enthusiasm. "My apartment is the size of a postage stamp. Is yours like that, too?"

I'm saved from answering because we've reached Chloe's destination. I stop the car at the front doors and put it into park.

"Thanks for the ride. I owe you." She puts a hand on my wrist, and it's like a thousand jolts of adrenaline shoot up my arm. She jerks her hand away and flexes her fingers like she's been stung. We stare at each other. She's the first to break the link between us by glancing out the window to the people crowding the sidewalk. "Maybe I'll see you around the building sometime." She gathers her purse and climbs out of the car.

"Yeah. Maybe."

I'm disappointed to see her go. Although we've just met, I'm drawn to her friendly manner and sunny smile. "Hey, can I give you some advice?"

"Sure. What?" She bends down to look inside the car, giving me a view all the way down her shirt to the lacy cups of her white bra.

"Don't accept any more rides from strangers, okay?"

"Okay. Got it." Her tits bob with her laughter. I glance away. I hate guys that ogle women. With a smile, she shuts the car door behind her.

I watch her walk around the front of the car and toward the building. Her ass is round and perfect. I adjust my cock behind the fly of my jeans. I'm full-on hard and ready to go. But not with her. Not with anyone inside my apartment building.

At the front door, she pauses to wave. The warmth of her smile chases away the chill of the rain. I smile and wave back. Maybe rules were made to be broken.

Just to be clear, I like to fuck. A lot. It's one of the reasons I'm so successful in my business. If a woman needs me to ride her all night and into the morning, my dick is more than happy to comply. Oral, anal, roleplay, kink, threesomes, couples—I'm down with it all. Most of my customers want standard missionary with a side helping of foreplay and pillow talk thrown into the mix. Whatever gets their rocks off. Makes no difference to me as long as they pay cash—in advance.

Mrs. Smith says she likes it rough, so I decide to dress like a biker for our date. After a light supper, I throw on my favorite pair of ripped jeans, heavy combat boots, and a tight white T-shirt beneath a black leather jacket. I don't bother to shave, choosing the scruffy, just-got-out-of-bed look, and muss my hair up with some gel. Appearances are everything in this line of work. I can't be a hard-ass dressed in a pink polo and khakis.

My dick's been semi-erect all day at the prospect of meeting a new client. I'm anxious, but looking forward to it all the same. Before leaving, I throw a box of condoms into a leather backpack, a couple different kinds of lube, mouthwash, and a vibrator—because, well, you never know when you might need one. Some women are difficult to get off the first time, and even I need a little help.

There's no shame in a bit of battery-operated assistance now and then.

As I leave my apartment and ride the elevator downstairs, my mind scrolls through a few different scenarios. I rehearse them in my head, paying no attention to the other occupants until Chloe boards the elevator on the fourth floor. She's wearing a short denim skirt, cowboy boots, and a tight blue T-shirt. When her gaze catches mine, she smiles, and I forget about Mrs. Smith. Fuck me, if this girl isn't the hottest thing I've seen in a long time. Her hair is swept into a high ponytail. She's the perfect combination of sweet and sexy.

"Howdy, partner," I say.

"Howdy." Her smile widens.

"Hot date?"

"Sort of. You?" Her gaze drifts over my body. I can tell by the way her nostrils flare she appreciates my bad boy outfit. Nothing tempts a good girl like a dirty, sexy bastard.

"Something like that." I shove my hands into my pockets and grin, thinking of the arsenal of erotic weapons slung over my shoulder. This Pollyanna would probably shit if she knew where I was really going. She tugs her lower lip between her teeth, drawing my focus to her mouth. Her lips are plump and tinted a soft rose color. A vision of them wrapped around my dick flashes through my head. I shake it away.

The elevator doors open, and we go our separate ways. She meets a skinny, bookish kind of guy at the lobby. He lights up at the sight of her, but it's me her eyes follow as I push through the revolving door and out onto the street.

***

Thirty minutes later, I park my car in the driveway of an austere three-story brick mansion on Dayton Street in Lincoln Park. The house is dark except for a few lights on the ground floor. I make my way up a sidewalk lined with frothy pink flowers and landscape lights. Once I reach the front door, I ring the doorbell and draw in a deep breath to get into character. Show time.

The woman who answers the door is petite, blonde, closer to fifty than forty. She's dressed in a floor-length satin robe tied tightly around her waist. Her hand trembles as she offers it to me.

"Hi, I'm Mrs. Smith. You must be—?" She frowns. "I don't know your name."

"Romeo," I say.

"Is that really your name?" she asks.

"Does it matter?" I lift an eyebrow and coax a smile from her.

"Not really." She steps aside to let me enter the foyer. I take in the two-story ceiling, crystal chandeliers, and marble floors. Very nice. Understated. Elegant but not fussy. I wait at the base of a double staircase. Her oval face has gone pale. "Should we go upstairs?" A tremor shakes her voice. "I'm not sure how this works."

"Why don't we sit down and chat for a minute? Your time won't start until we're both ready."

"Okay then. Yes. Let's get acquainted first." She breathes a sigh of relief and leads the way into an expansive living room. "Would you like a drink?"

"No, thanks. But go ahead if you'd like." I take a seat on the sofa, sling my backpack to the floor, and watch as she heads to the wet bar a few feet away. Ice tinkles into a rock glass. She pours two fingers of bourbon over the ice, takes a sip, then another. Her shoulders visibly relax.

I never drink during work hours. Too many things might go wrong, in which case, I need my wits about me. You never know when a husband or boyfriend might arrive home unexpectedly. I've had to launch out a bedroom window and hightail it down the street to safety more than once. It's also a well-known fact that alcohol can inhibit sexual performance. My customers expect satisfaction, and I expect to give it to them—no pun intended—something I can't do with a whiskey dick.

"Have you been doing this long?" She turns to face me. The

lamp from the bar backlights her figure. The outlines of her body show through the thin silk. Perky breasts, slender thighs, a flat belly. This will be an easy ride for me. It's always nice to see a woman take care of her body, although I have no preference on physical type. They all feel the same once you're inside, regardless of age or fitness level.

"A few years."

"You're younger than I expected." The liquor is making her brave. By the time she finishes her drink, she'll be ready to move upstairs.

"I'm twenty-four," I reply and pat the sofa beside me. "Have a seat." She eases onto the cushion next to me. The throat of her robe gapes open to reveal a sliver of smooth, tanned skin and the upper swell of one breast. I play with the hem of her robe and lean toward her.

"Does it bother you—the age difference?" Her breath catches as my fingers graze her knee.

"Not at all. I prefer older women. They know their bodies better, know what they want." That's the honest truth. Her eyes latch onto my mouth and hold there. I run my tongue over my lower lip to tease her.

"My friend said you were hot, but you're absolutely gorgeous. You must work out a lot." She takes another sip of her drink while her gaze slides over my chest, pupils widening.

I scoot a little closer, almost but not quite thigh to thigh. "Every day."

When her gaze drifts over my biceps, I'm grateful for the hundred or so push-ups and crunches I did before leaving my apartment. "I've been working on my abs this week. Would you like to see?"

"Yes." She's almost ready to begin, and so am I. The challenge turns me on, sends blood rushing into my cock.

"Great. Just a few details and then I'm going to take you upstairs and fuck you the way you deserve to be fucked." I grin and wink. She nods, her gaze trained on my face, and I continue. "Cash up front. Two-fifty for an hour. A grand for the night. Non-refundable."

"I've got the money for two hours here." She withdraws an envelope from the pocket of her robe and hands it to me. "And a bonus for working me into your schedule on such late notice."

I riffle through the bills then drop the money into my backpack. Later, I'll put the cash in my safe deposit box at the bank. I brush a lock of hair back from her face. Anticipation is a huge part of the process. She needs to want me. Taking a woman to ecstasy is as much a mental journey as physical.

"Oh, my God. This is really happening," she whispers. A flush creeps up her neck. Beneath her robe, her nipples poke against the fabric, tight and hard.

"If I see you out in public, I won't acknowledge you unless you speak to me first—and never when I'm with another client. Condoms are required and non-negotiable. I get tested regularly for STDs. Here's a copy of the results from the last test." I pull the paper from my backpack, hand it to her, and wait as she scans through the results. When she's done, I return the paper to my backpack. "I'll fuck you any way you want. You're in control of this situation. This is about you. If at any time you want to stop, just say the word and we're done. Understand?"

"Yes. I understand." She licks her lips like she's parched and I'm a cold drink of water. I live for looks like that. Maybe I didn't get enough attention from my mom as a kid, or maybe I just dig women.

With slow movements, I cup one of her breasts in my hand, lift it, and flick the nipple with my thumb. She hisses. The satin is soft in my palm. Her head falls back against the sofa. When I pinch her nipple between my fingers, a shudder ripples down her body and her eyelids lower. Fine lines bracket her eyes, spiderwebs of pain and experience. I lean forward and touch my lips to hers. The taste of bourbon burns my tongue.

When I pull back, she says, "I'm ready to go upstairs," in a voice thick with desire. I smile at her, because I'm ready, too.

3

COMPLICATIONS

When I come out of the bathroom the next morning, freshly showered, Mrs. Smith is still in bed, hair tangled and naked beneath the sheets. She looks thoroughly satisfied. She should. We fucked all night, well past the two-hour initial agreement. I gave her everything she wanted and then some. What can I say? I take serious pride in a job well done.

She watches me saunter across the room. I drop the towel at the foot of the bed and step into my jeans.

"You're amazing," she says. Her eyes linger on my chest as I pull the T-shirt over my head.

"Thanks. I'm glad you enjoyed it. I had a great time." I can't help but feel sorry for her. She's an attractive woman, trapped in a prison of social and political expectations. I see that a lot in my line of work —marriages based on status or money, devoid of feeling. It's not my place to judge, though, so I shake off the pity. She's an intelligent adult, and if she's unhappy, it's her own damn fault. I gave up trying to change people a long time ago. My job is to provide a service, not life coaching or counseling.

"Do you think we can do this again?" With the sheet clutched to her chest, she sits up.

I nod, happy to acquire another regular. "Sure. What did you have in mind?"

"The same time next week?" A flush creeps up her neck. "For the whole night?"

"Absolutely." I open the calendar on my phone and set up a standing appointment. I'll need to move a few things around, but the prospect of a thousand dollars for one night's work is worth the hassle.

"Are you hungry? Would you like some breakfast?" Her tone is hopeful, but her shoulders tense.

"This isn't a date. You don't have to treat me like one."

"Right." The strain fades from her posture. "I don't know why I said that."

"It's okay. I've been inside you. We shared something very intimate. Your body is teeming with endorphins and oxytocin that manipulate your emotions. It can get a little confusing."

"You're one of a kind, Romeo." A smile returns to her lips.

"You got that right." I wink, give her a peck on the cheek, and stare into her eyes. It adds a personal touch and warms the coldness of our business transaction. "Don't get up. Stay in bed. Relax. I'll show myself out."

"Do you mind?" Another blush colors her cheeks. "I don't think I'll be able to walk for a week."

"Better get used to it. I went easy on you this time." I laugh and grab my backpack as I go. "Take a warm bath and some ibuprofen. It'll help."

"Okay. I will." She wraps her arms around her knees. With the first rays of dawn streaming through the windows, she looks younger, rejuvenated. "Romeo?"

I pause, hand on the doorknob. "Yeah?"

"Thank you."

"My pleasure." As I walk out the door, the sun is peeking over the horizon. A profound sense of emptiness fills my chest, the way it always does after a date. During sex, I disconnect from my emotions and concentrate on the physical sensations. Like I told her, the flood of chemicals that accompany sex can wreak havoc on a person if they aren't careful. Developing feelings for a client would be a catastrophe. For my mental safety, I have to remain impartial and detached. I didn't used to be that way, but now the coldness consumes me. I feel it licking at my heels, chasing my humanity like a rabid wolf. I'm scared for the boy I used to be and the heartless man I'm becoming.

I shove aside the discontent, focus on the growling engine of my sexy car and the horizon. By the colors of the sky, it's going to be a beautiful day. I scroll through a mental checklist of tasks to complete over the next twelve hours. The gym, manicure, haircut, tanning bed...the list is endless. But before anything, I need to schedule a few hours of sleep.

Back at my apartment, I dive into bed. I'm deep into dreamland when a thunderous knocking at the door sends my heart into my throat. The walls shake with the force of the pounding. I stagger out of bed, naked, and into the foyer. When I glance through the peephole, the face on the other side sends a shiver of dread up my spine. I open the door.

"Here." Shonda shoves our daughter into my arms, oblivious to my nudity, and drops the diaper bag at my bare feet. In spite of my irritation, I smile at the round, pink face of my daughter Madison staring back at me from the bundle of blankets.

"What are you doing?" The words are barely out of my mouth when Shonda spins on her heels and marches down the hall. I call after her, the baby balanced in the crook of my arm. "It's only Tuesday. I don't have her until next week."

"Well, you've got her now." Shonda stabs the elevator button. I pad after her, my bare ass on display for the world to see.

"You can't just drop her here. I've got shit going on tonight. You can't keep doing this." We stare at each other. Animosity thickens the air between us. We're two strangers bound by the common bond of a child. Shonda is the reason I don't have sex with non-paying women. A one-night stand after a night of clubbing and a defective condom has tied me to a woman I can't stand for eternity.

Don't get me wrong. I love this baby girl more than my own life. She's the one good thing I've created. But Shonda has a habit of dropping Maddie on my doorstep then disappearing for days at a time. I have no idea where she goes or what she does. The haggard circles beneath her eyes and the way her clothing hangs on her skeletal frame suggest she's on a downward spiral—again.

"I can't take it anymore." Shonda's voice shakes. "I need a break."

I draw in a deep breath and try to remain calm. "I get it. I'm happy to watch her, but you can't just dump her on me without a little advance notice. When are you coming back?"

Shonda's brown eyes wander around the hall, disconnected and hazy, avoiding my gaze. "Tomorrow. I just need a little time to get my head together." She runs a frail hand through the disheveled mess of her hair. "Tomorrow. I'll be back tomorrow."

"Okay. What time?" I bounce Maddie in my arms to ease the frown on my chubby face.

The elevator doors open. Shonda steps inside.

"What time will you pick her up?"

"Tomorrow," she says with a vague wave of her hand.

The elevator doors shut, and I'm left standing naked in the hallway with a nine-month-old baby in my arms. After I return to my apartment, I do what any self-respecting man does when faced with an insurmountable problem. I call my mom.

4

FAMILY MATTERS

Maddie snuffles against my neck. I take her to the sofa where we cuddle for the next thirty minutes. I'm so tired I can barely keep my eyes open, but she's wide awake, her frown replaced by a wide smile. Her chubby feet kick against my belly. I blow raspberries on the bottom of her foot. She shrieks with delight.

These are the moments I cherish the most in my life, the ones with my baby girl, just the two of us. Even before the paternity test, there was no denying she's my kid. Thick, wavy black hair covers the top of her round head, and brown eyes follow my every move. By the length of her body and legs, she's going to be tall like me.

"Dadadadada," she says.

"What was that?" My heart jumps. I lift her to stand on my legs, bracing her beneath the armpits. She bobbles up and down, bending at the knees like a drunken party girl in a nightclub.

"Dadadada," she replies, and it's the best damn day of my life.

Overwhelming love swells inside my chest until my ribs creak. I pepper kisses on her forehead and nose. Her fat fingers latch onto the leather necklace tied around my neck and yank as she tries to shove it into her mouth.

"Daddy loves you, baby girl," I tell her. "Don't you ever forget that."

After breakfast, we take a short nap then I give her a bath. She splashes water all over me, giggling at my funny faces. While I change clothes, she crawls over the floor of my bedroom with the speed of a rabbit. By the time I have on my jeans and a T-shirt, I'm sweaty and out of breath from chasing her. I hoist her up to my chest and head to the elevator. Thank goodness, my mom is available to babysit for a few hours.

Chloe loiters in the lobby. She's wearing strappy sandals, faded jeans, and a halter top that shows off her gorgeous tits. Her eyes brighten at the sight of us.

"Oh, my goodness. Who is this? Is she yours? She's adorable," Chloe exclaims. Maddie extends a hand to Chloe then buries her face in my neck, overcome with shyness.

"Yeah, this is my daughter, Maddie." I'm aware of the effect a guy with a baby has on a woman. Chloe's not immune. Her full lips curve into a wide smile. For a second, I'm transfixed by the combination of her sun-kissed skin, white teeth, and long brown hair. "We're going to run some errands."

"Well, I won't keep you then. Have a nice time." She waves to Maddie, who curls and uncurls her fist in goodbye. My hand is on the door when Chloe calls after us. "Hey, um, if you're not doing anything later, why don't you stop by—both of you? I'm going to babysit for my niece tonight. She's about Maddie's age. We can hang out, watch TV while they play. I'm in 4B."A hopeful note lilts her voice. She's standing near the window, and a shaft of light illuminates undertones of gold and auburn in her hair.

I don't have a lot of friends, none with children. Part of me wants to accept the offer. Another part of me recoils in fear. I can't risk exposing my occupation to Chloe. Maddie gurgles and digs her

fingers into my hair. Looking at her angelic face causes me to recon-
sider. Maybe I don't need friends, but she does. All I want is for her
to be happy. It's the reason I fuck strange women for money, and the
reason I'm desperate to have full custody of her.

"Okay. What time?" I disentangle the baby's hand from my hair.

"Really? How about six? I'll order a pizza or something." A
dimple deepens on the left side of her mouth.

"Sure. We'll be there, but I'll bring the pizza. See you then." No
matter how hard I try, I can't pry my eyes away from Chloe's lips, the
way her tongue glides over them like she's thirsty. With great self-
control, I force my feet in the direction of the street.

From the kitchen of her house, Ma sweeps aside the curtains
above the sink and frowns at my car parked in her driveway
of her suburban home. She's wearing yoga pants and a tight
cropped T-shirt that shows off her flat belly. At forty-two, she's too
young to have a grandkid. Something she likes to remind me of at
every opportunity. Smoke curls from the cigarette in her hand and
floats around her head. She stubs it out in an overflowing ashtray. She
knows I hate her smoking around Maddie.

"Where on God's green earth did that come from?" She turns
brown eyes, eyes identical to mine and Maddie's, to greet me. I open
my mouth to concoct a lie, but she waves a hand between us. "Never
mind. I don't want to know." Her forehead furrows. "You're not
dealing drugs, are you?"

"No, Ma. Scout's honor." I hold up my hands, palms facing
outward, and put on my best innocent face.

She shakes her head and shoves back the hair from my forehead,
the same way she did when I was a boy. "Good. You've got a kid to
think about." As she speaks, she bends to smile at Maddie, safely
strapped into the baby carrier on the kitchen table. Her grand-

daughter kicks her feet and coos. "Your daddy's a dumb ass, sweet pea." Maddie laughs.

"Traitor." I take my daughter from the carrier and hold her up in front of me. Warmth swells inside me, like a bubble about to burst. She's growing so fast. I drop a kiss on her nose. "Thanks for watching her, Ma. I'll be back by four."

"You better be." Mom lights up another cigarette. "I've got a date tonight."

"Who's the lucky guy? Anyone I know?"

"Gary from the bowling alley." She lights another cigarette.

"Mom." I scowl. "I don't want Maddie around all that smoke."

"Sorry. Back when you were a kid, no one cared about this stuff." She sighs and carefully extinguishes the cigarette, which she will probably light up again as soon as I leave.

"Here's a little something to get you by." I set an envelope with four hundred dollars on the counter. It's not much, but it's enough to keep her rent paid for another month.

"Thanks, babe." She sweeps the envelope off the counter and into the drawer. "You know, as long as you're passing out the cash, your sister could use a little help."

"We've been over this a million times, Ma. I'm not giving her any money. She'll just give it to her loser boyfriend." It's not that I don't love Mona. I do. With all my heart. Her loser boyfriend, however, spends more time in jail than out. "You're enabling her."

"It's not enabling. It's unconditional love." Her face puckers into an irritated pout. "You'll understand once Maddie gets bigger. She's going to make mistakes, but you won't be able to turn your back on her."

"Maddie isn't going to date felons. She's going to be a doctor or a lawyer or something fantastic, aren't you, princess?" I tweak Maddie's toes, delighting in her bubbling laughter. Although my tone is light-hearted, I've never been more serious about anything. My girl deserves the best life has to offer.

"There you go again with those crazy, pie-in-the-sky notions." Ma shakes her head. She crosses her arms over her chest and stares out the window above the sink at the uninspiring view of the neighbor's broken privacy fence. "Why can't you be happy with what you've got instead of moving into the city, getting into Lord knows what kind of trouble?"

"I'm grateful for everything I've got. That doesn't mean I can't want better for my kid." I bite my lower lip to keep from saying more. We've had this argument a dozen times, and it always ends in hurt feelings on both sides.

"I blame that university for putting foolish notions in your head. We're a blue collar, working-class family. Your daddy was a garbage man, and your granddaddy worked in the factory for forty odd years. There's no shame in hard work. The sooner you realize your place in the world, the better off you'll be." A note of despondence flattens her tone. I try not to blame her for being a pessimist. She never had the means or opportunity to leave this squalid neighborhood.

I tried a factory job and lasted exactly three days in the hot, dirty assembly line of an automotive parts supplier. "I don't belong here, Ma. There's more to life than Riverdale."

"I'll take your word for it." The tight line of her lips signals that this conversation is over.

"And that's my cue to leave." I hand Maddie over to Ma. "I changed her right before we got here, and she's already had breakfast, so she should be ready for a nap soon."

"I've raised two kids on my own. We'll be fine. Won't we, sweetheart?" Her previous irritation melts away the second her granddaughter reaches for her.

I brush the hair from Maddie's forehead and give her one last kiss. "I'll be back in a little bit. Be good for Grammy, okay?"

"Go on. Get out of here." Ma angles her face away from me and taps her cheek, signaling for a kiss.

Outside, I pause to scrutinize my childhood home. The eaves are filled with sprouting weeds. One of the windows has been boarded over instead of replaced, and the porch steps are broken. The peeling paint and overgrown yard contrast with the sleek, expensive shape of the Lexus parked in the driveaway. Someday, I'm going to have enough money to get my ma a nice house in a safe neighborhood. Even if I have to fuck all of Chicago to make it happen.

SPECIAL DELIVERY

At the top of the Belfast building, I enter the reception area of Armand Investments and pause to turn the brim of my baseball cap to the back. Pizza box in hand, I maneuver through the lobby and into the elevator. The scent of pepperoni and spices causes my mouth to water. My thoughts stray to Chloe. I forgot to ask what kind of pizza she likes for our playdate tonight. I'd call her, but I don't have her number. I don't know anything about her, really. The elevator dings and the doors slide open at the fifty-first floor.

"Delivery for Ms. Armand," I tell the receptionist.

She leads me down a long, silent corridor. Her heels click on the cold marble floor. At the end of the hall, she knocks on heavy wood doors then pushes them open. Ms. Armand sits behind an enormous glass and steel desk. A wall of windows offers a panoramic view of the city behind her. It's an unusually clear day. Lake Michigan is visible in the distance, its surface dotted with tiny sailboats and enormous freighters.

"I've got your pizza here," I say. The receptionist hovers, but I keep my gaze trained on the woman behind the desk.

"That will be all, Mary." Ms. Armand doesn't look up from the computer screen. Her dark hair is slicked into an elegant twist at the nape of her neck. Sunlight illuminates a few red-gold strands, reminding me of Chloe. I push away her memory, determined to concentrate on my customer. Once the door closes behind the receptionist, Ms. Armand stands and straightens the waistband of her skirt. She's tall and leggy. The lines of her suit emphasize large breasts and a tiny waist. Her blue eyes meet mine. A bolt of attraction zings straight to my dick. I love this freaking job.

"That'll be fifteen dollars." I hold the pizza out to her.

"You can set it there." She nods to the coffee table and sofa beside us. "I'm sorry. I don't seem to have any money. Could I put this on my tab?"

"That's not gonna work." I fight to stay in character. "What're we going to do about this?" Her gaze never leaves mine. It's full of heat.

"Maybe we can work something out." She stalks toward me, putting an extra swing into her hips.

"I need my cash, lady." Manicured fingers climb up the buttons on my shirt. She's close enough that I can see the pulse flutter in her neck. Her perfume, floral and light, reminds me of the park down the street from my apartment building.

"Isn't there some other way I can pay you?" She bats thick, black lashes and sweeps her tongue over her lower lip.

"You could let me fuck you." I would never talk to a woman this way in real life, but the fantasy is a total turn-on. "Or you could suck my cock. Either one is fine with me." To be fair, I feel guilty for charging a woman to give me a blow job, but some women are into it.

"Oh, no, I couldn't do that." She feigns shock, her red lips forming an O.

I grab her hands. "The way I see it, you don't have a choice." I shove her against the window. Her back thuds against the glass. "What's your choice? Fucking or sucking?" I lean into her, pinning her wrists over her head, and draw the tip of my nose along the line of her jaw. The full curves of her breasts rise and fall between us. "I'm good either way."

"Fucking." The word is a groan torn from her lips.

"Fucking it is. Turn around. Palms on the window." I run a hand up the inside of her thigh. She's wearing stockings. My fingertips glide over garter straps before hitting pay dirt. The cotton panel of her panties is soaked. I twist a finger in the elastic and rip away the scrap of lace. Next, I grip her jaw in my hand, turning her face to the side, demanding her attention. "You're going to be quiet while I take what you owe me. We wouldn't want your employees to know what a bad girl you are. Not a peep, understand?"

She nods. I drag a finger over the slippery, drenched folds of her sex. Her body trembles. Using my knee as a wedge, I part her legs. The growl of my zipper fills the silence. My cock throbs at this exciting game. Damn, I love role play.

"Don't move." I pull away from her long enough to put on a condom. With one rough thrust, I penetrate her. We both moan. Her pussy clenches around me. I begin to move, sliding in and out of her. Our bodies slap together. She whimpers but doesn't speak. I pretend she's Chloe. That it's Chloe I'm fucking in the middle of the day, high above Chicago.

"Ah, so good," the woman mutters.

"Shut up. Did I say you can speak?" I warn her and slap her on the ass before doubling the pace. Is Chloe this tight, I wonder? Does she moan? The idea excites me even more. Hot fire races through my veins. My balls ache with the need to come. The shaft of my cock slips and slides through Ms. Armand's wet channel.

"Yes. That's good," she says. Her voice is rough and broken. "Use me."

"You'll never try to cheat me again. Understand?" I fist a hand in her hair. She growls with pleasure.

"I do. I understand." Her composure dissolves. I push into her hard, filling her with my hardness, and hold still, making her beg. "No, no. Please don't stop."

"You like it too much." The pause gives me time to hold back what promises to be an epic orgasm.

"I know. I do. I'm a dirty whore." Glassy blue eyes stare over her shoulder. Patches of pink color her cheeks. I pull out. She whimpers in dismay. "I promise to be good. Just don't stop. Please."

"I thought I told you to be quiet." If anyone outside the office can hear us, I'm sure they're shocked. The idea puts a grin on my face. She frowns, and I drop the smile. "Don't look at me. Eyes front."

I penetrate her with a commanding thrust. Her pussy quivers and tightens. We both sigh at the exquisite friction. She likes it dirty. So do I. This shared fantasy makes her one of my favorite customers. If I wasn't a gigolo and she wasn't a man-hater, I'd do her for free.

"I'm going to make you come now. And I don't want to hear a single noise from your pretty mouth." I grab her ass with both hands and pick up a new rhythm.

Pressure builds between us. She's sopping wet. My thrusts are sloppy but controlled. My fingers tighten on the white flesh of her ass while I try to time my release with hers. Her legs begin to shake. I drive deeper, pounding the hell out of her. Our heaving breaths fill the room. She bites her lower lip to stay quiet and comes hard. The contractions of her pussy trigger my orgasm. I slam into her one last time, spilling my load into the rubber. The relief is instantaneous and welcome.

I brace a hand on the window above her shoulder. My knees are weak. It takes a few seconds before I can withdraw and stand upright. Ms. Armand drops to her knees. With a trembling hand, she pushes the hair back from her face then blows out a lungful of air.

"That was freaking amazing. You never disappoint me, Romeo." Her smile illuminates her blue eyes. "Your money's on the desk." She nods toward the white envelope next to her computer.

"This was the best one yet. The pizza delivery was a great idea. I don't know how you'll top this." I extend a hand to help her stand.

She pulls her skirt down over her hips. Her cheeks are flushed, eyes wild. I release her hand and go for the condom. While I dispose of the evidence, she moves to the connecting bathroom to clean up.

"Oh, I've got something interesting up my sleeve for next time." She pops her head out of the door to give me a wink. "Don't you worry. Just keep that enormous cock of yours at the ready."

"I can hardly wait." Of all my customers, she's the one closest to my age. Fucking her is more pleasure than work. I almost—*almost*—feel guilty about taking her money. As I thumb through the envelope of twenty dollar bills, I change my mind. One hundred bucks for fifteen minutes of work. I grin back at her. My life rocks.

Don't like cliffhangers? Then stop reading here. If you want more, then keep going.

Two hours later, I'm back at my apartment building, showered and shaved. Nervous perspiration coats my palms when I knock on Chloe's door. I'm confident when working, but it's been a long time since I met a woman for anything but sex. Not to mention the overwhelming guilt of fucking a client while picturing Chloe's face. This chemical attraction has to end for both our sakes.

Maddie rests against my chest, her chubby arms tight about my neck. Her innocent touch brings me back to reality. I'm gonna eat some pizza, let Maddie socialize, and get the hell out.

My plan shatters when Chloe answers the door. For a blinding moment, I'm lost in her genuine warmth and unassuming smile. She's wearing gray yoga pants and an oversized pink T-shirt with *Princess* spelled in sequins over the chest. I can see the outline of her bra. Her nipples point at me through the thin cotton. My dick twitches in appreciation while my self-control groans.

"I'm doing this for you, baby," I murmur into Maddie's hair. "It's going to be a long night for daddy."

Don't miss the next steamy episode of Bad Behavior. Get Bad Behavior #2 now.